THE YEAR I WENT AWAY

JORGE SCHNEIDER

THE YEAR I WENT AWAY

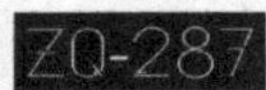

The Year I Went Away

Published by
ZQ-287 Press
Long Beach, CA

Gracias infinitas a Steven Bramble, quien siempre creyó en mi y en mi trabajo. Y cuyos consejos construyeron un mejor libro.

ISBN:
Paintings by: Jorge Schneider
Cover and Interior Design: Steven T. Bramble

to Alejandra

for being my dawn and my dusk

THE YEAR I WENT AWAY

JORGE SCHNEIDER

*TRANSLATED FROM THE SPANISH
IN COLLABORATION WITH THE AUTHOR
BY*
STEVEN T. BRAMBLE

LONG BEACH   OAKLAND

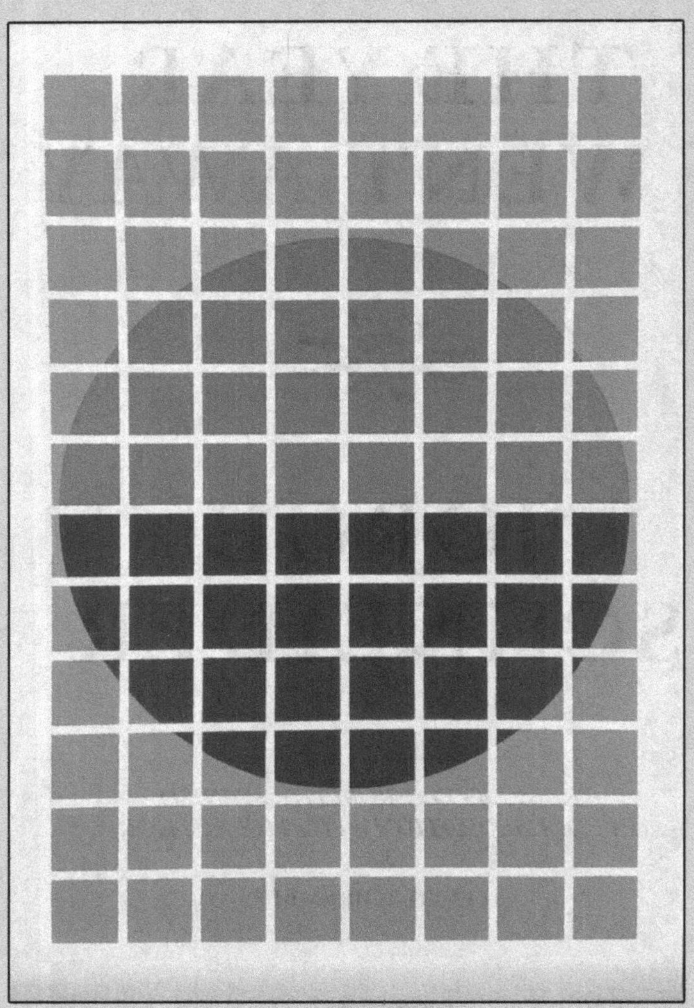

I

Fourteen days. Three hundred thirty-six hours. To the dot—not one more or less. The clock in my head advances and I'm yet to find a place to live. For the time being I'm sleeping at the pension on Calle Defensa, a few blocks from the financial district, where everyone runs like crazy one place to another wearing stern, tense, worried expressions. Though you might not believe it, there are some who describe that swirl of faces as being composed of mature, trustworthy individuals, dutiful to their institution and admirable in their sangfroid. There's a bit of truth to that, I guess. Some of those individuals, I know from experience, do not succumb to so much as a bit of good humor, even should the moment call for it. I see them. I track them with my eyes every morning during my walk down Calle 25 de Mayo, in search of some encouraging face that might give me a push forward, a reason not to get bogged down in the swamp of my days. The endless procession of cold eyes isn't what bothers me, rather the power they carry, the power of decision held by grown children, the power to decide for others—the reality of it gives me chills, makes me feel suffocated in their milieu. I arrive at Reconquista, head towards Retiro, emerge onto Avenida Libertador with its chasmal width, immense as the gap separating me from the inhabitants of these opulent towers and their view of the river.

Two weeks. Not a day more. I have to be out by the first of the month. In the same confusing hurry as always, I gave advance notice of my departure, certain I would soon find something better than the tiny cell at the pension. But Buenos Aires is packed full like a bus at rush hour, bodies spilling over seats into the aisles, hanging out the windows, crawling roofwards with jagged fingernails… in the streets people roam about with the modest intention of finding a place to lie down and sleep for the night. Plaza Houssay on Avenida Córdoba is a permanent parking lot of humanity all pissing and shitting outdoors while encircled by luxury high-rises.

Just three months ago I was a financier. Every day for five years, dressed in suits, I kissed my wife Susana goodbye and was lost among the workforce in subways and cafes. I made a good living as one of those grown children. My initial foray in college had been philosophy, but it had quickly churned up an inner chaos, a souring toward myself and others, toward life itself. Anywhere I looked I couldn't find my footing. I became ten, twelve, fifteen, eighty-seven minds, too many to keep track of. So instead I made the decision to be no mind at all. I gave myself over to numbers and routine. I marched ahead with my life in the most controlled and resolute way I knew how.

On Saturdays Susana and I would head to the club for tennis and cocktails. At night she would apply excessive makeup, drape herself in expensive clothes—a good upper-middle-class woman ready to impress her circle. We would go to the theater or cinema, then to dinner. The play or movie was beside the point—we went to be *seen*, to be normal, to fill the time. Sundays, at Susana's urging, belonged to Father Javier and his sermons. I saw in her the same tendency I had encountered in everyone in matters of worship since childhood. She was convinced of the social value of the church, not of her own faith. Going to mass was like going to a game of canasta, greetings here, kisses there, and then, in view of everyone, the opportunity to show one's charitable side by palming off a few pesos to some poor wretch. But I didn't judge; I didn't think. I went along. The weekend inevitably ended with Susana lying on her back on the sheets of our bed, my body pressed against her, swaying to the rhythm of her moans. Once finished we would shower and fall asleep as if nothing had ever happened. Our love, if it ever existed, was a long distant memory, an echo fading with successive distance. We divorced at the beginning of December. Not having children made things simpler, but she kept the condo on Avenida Las Heras, along with the art we'd accumulated for years. Only a day later I left my job for good—or was run out of it, depending which side of the burning bridge you were on.

Since then I've been doing odd jobs, things of minimal responsibility or difficulty, keeping up the books of a few local businesses and occasionally helping an old friend of mine who paints houses in the posh southern part of Buenos Aires. I've yet to miss my career. That frantic world of interest rates, obscure news, tea-leaf readers, maniacal personalities; I need something more human. Some other way of living, at least; it was no longer possible to march ahead blindly, living under the twin command of Money and God. Stendhal said God's only excuse is he doesn't exist. As for Money, well, much like the clergy, my purpose had been to keep certain sacred notions alive. But I've stripped myself of all that. I'm looking for something different. In psychological terms, I'm seeking a breakthrough. From the point of view of others, I've experienced a breakdown. I wish I could say any of it was intentional.

I'd like to find a place in San Telmo despite the

tourists. I can't see myself on Avenida Libertador. This is probably an impulse to speed along the undeterrable fate of becoming working class. A perhaps crude but true statement is that I've never fit in well with working class people, and especially not working-class politics, either right- or left-wing. I was accused of this most often at university, by other middle-class students like me, but I was merely being honest when I said I couldn't see collective freedom as anything other than a methodical assassination of individual liberty. A man without a responsible ego seems to me nothing more than a robotic idiot, though this frequently provoked outrage in the hardline Peronistas[†] as well as the communists. I retrace my steps and cross Plaza de Mayo, its stone monuments graffitied with slogans set against deaf and barricaded government buildings. I turn onto Avenida Paseo Colón, Avenida Independencia, past Calle Bolívar to Calle Perú. Here I run across a refurbished warehouse, turned into lofts. There's a handwritten sign outside: ROOM FOR RENT. I ring the bell and wait, finding I'm a bit nervous.

The heavy iron gate creaks open, accompanied by a pant of exertion.

"Sorry, this door is so heavy…" A slender woman with curly black hair stands before me, eyes, too, black

[†] Juan Domingo Perón was president of Argentina from 1946-1955, and again from 1973-74. He spearheaded a dictatorial, quasi-fascist political party which still holds immense influence in the country, though its ideology has morphed to serve different purposes.

as ebony. She's beautiful.

"Can I help you?" she asks.

"I saw you have a room available?"

"It's 18,000 pesos a month. First two months in advance."

"Okay. And when is rent usually due?"

"Between the first and the sixth."

"Mind if I take a look?"

I follow her up a granite staircase framed by a balustrade of huge blocks of Carrara marble. At the top she opens the interior door, another heavy one of wrought iron and beveled glass. The place is as huge as it is eclectic, massive arched windows with oversized sills usable as benches. The space is divided into several sections by makeshift partitions, bookshelves, sculptures. The original walls are exposed brick. There seems to be a garden or patio towards the back. A spiral staircase of spindly black iron leads to a mezzanine full of books and canvases.

"You're a painter?" I ask.

"Every now and then."

"A reader, too, I see."

"Sometimes."

"I'm Julio Von Artens."

"Jezebel. Nice to meet you."

"Just Jezebel?"

"Just Jezebel."

She goes and leans against the wall in the corner. I do a quick walkthrough. I like it. Despite a tinge of melancholy, something about it gives me a good feeling.

"Anyone else interested?" I ask.

"Not yet. We just put the sign up this morning. You're the first."

"We?"

"Antonio and me. That's his studio up there. He's the painter," she says. "Also an actor."

"So there would be three of us."

"Four. Abel's away on business."

"I see…"

"You'd be up in the studio. The only thing is, whenever Antonio's painting you'll have to move down here. He'll only paint up in the loft. He likes the heights." She spins her finger around next to her temple—*cuckoo*. "Artists, you know. What do you do, Julio?"

I hesitate, unsure what to tell her.

"Is it a secret?"

"I'm… Well, I *was*… in finance…"

"In *this* poor country?"

I shrug.

She looks at the ground, supremely incredulous and calm. "Anything's possible, I guess. I don't know if this would really work out for you, though. Antonio's crazy, Abel's in and out all the time, and I'm… well, the point is, you're a banker."

"I *was* in finance," I correct. "*Was*. I'll take it."

It's her turn to hesitate, thinking for a moment with a fingernail in her mouth. "Fine, I suppose. It's your funeral. But you need to know Antonio paints any time of the day or night."

"What do you mean?"

"Like I said. He goes up and starts painting whenever he feels like." She gestures hopelessly. "He's like that. That's why I say, if you're used to stability and routine, it may not be the best choice."

Now that I think of it, this does seem inconvenient. On the other hand, it's the first bit of luck I've had searching for an apartment, and given my lack of time and the intriguing nature of the place…

"I'll take it," I say. "The room or study or whatever you've got."

"Okay, then."

"Great. Is it possible to move in tomorrow?"

"I don't see why not."

We clarify a few more details and she walks me out.

I head toward the river. The morning opens like a gray overcoat. People flood the streets, a sea of fine crystal revolving doors knotted with crowds, the city's murmuring constant, comforting and oppressive. I hurry against the surging legion of jaded faces. Jezebel, how can that be her name? It has to be a sobriquet; what parent would forsake a child to a sensually charged label like that? A car horn blares and someone tells the driver to fuck off. My mind remains fixed on her, bearer of that tired but unexhausted stare. Circling the Casa Rosada[†] onto Calle Florida, I'm frozen in astonishment when a poor eight-year-old boy approaches me with hand out-stretched—his eyes are exactly those of Jezebel. How is it possible? They're the same eyes in all but deportment. His are not simply weary but empty, unbearably empty, wells of Cimmerian blackness down which his soul has encountered an endless falling. He asks for pesos, but I can't, I can't give him anything. I dodge him, doing my best to shake off the uncanny similarity. I'm not normally superstitious, but for a moment this seems a sign I should maybe just keep my place at the pension. Did that kid ever even have an option before losing his future? Or did he lose it gradually, like snow melting under sunlight?

I stop at a bar on the corner, taking a seat by the window. Revolving a spoon in a cortado[‡], my unease fades and it finally hits me I've just found a new place. Living in a painter's studio should be interesting, if nothing else. What was his name? I don't remember. I sip the coffee and do my best to block out the Tuesday unfolding all around me. A whole month already since I threw my watch in the trash. I was a slave to it for years. Come to think of it, I don't remember where I bought

---

† Seat of the Argentine executive branch.

‡ A shot of espresso with a small amount of milk and foam.

it, though I remember its beautiful Roman numerals that one day abducted me and never let go. I still see its face in my mind, doing all it can to hang on, keep me obedient. I look around. Every person here has a watch. Fine, expensive time pieces that look fine and expensive near the hand. The condemned introducing their executioners with pride.

Susana loved clocks. The bigger the better. Pendulums devouring hours and days was, for her, the most delicious kind of satisfaction. We had one made of pine in the dining room that marked the hours with single-note chimes. Those chimes terrified me. On more than one occasion they entered my dreams. They made the house reverberate very slightly each time with their frequency. Every hour it was a renewed feeling of having something stolen from you, like life itself was meted out through the thing's ceaseless gears. I couldn't understand her fascination. She couldn't understand my horror. There was something immature about my dislike of clocks, she said. The street fills with the lunch hour crowd, office workers everywhere, clusters of women with ripped stockings and heels clattering on the broken tiles of downtown sidewalks. Men with lines under their eyes, women with smudged makeup, cigarettes in shaking hands. I recognize these things, every aspect of this form of living. Now, apart from it but amongst it, I fail to see the wisdom. I find it interesting to observe them, like watching forgotten moments of a past life. Young women who order cheap coffee or pastry. Many eat in silence, eyes lost and hazy. They're not empty yet. They still have hope something will happen in their lives, because how can it be that in the end nothing happens? Then there are the men, the usual porteños†, noisy and demanding like no one else in the world. They complain about everything and smoke. They smoke like hell. The only thing more abundant than cigarettes is foul language. The average waitress is a masterpiece of stoicism when these men order what they want how they want it, often followed by some coarse compliment. At the bar, next to the cash register, like an older version of myself, sits a gray-haired fifty-year-old, elbow on the counter, chin in fist, observing everything.

In the space of a day I'll be going from lonely as an oyster to living in a house full of people. How will loneliness feel in the company of strangers? It's been a long time since I've had roommates. The arrangement is ridiculous, but I wanted something different, so why not? For the first time in a lifetime, I'm free to pursue the unknown.

The lunch rush ends. I watch a world of eager faces returning to take calls, make spreadsheets, retail cell phone cases. There's a saying that work dignifies people. In that case, what do people themselves dignify? Or

---

† Person who lives in Buenos Aires.

are we incapable of dignifying anything? If not, then I will be both undignified and undignifying. I've made that decision. I'm tired of all this nonstop running, of keeping myself busy, swamped even, for the purpose of marching ahead and letting the clock eat hours. The end of Susana and me, the end of my career—how did it all happen?—it doesn't even matter—it was an invitation to enter a life that rejects time.

II

"Is that everything, Julio?"

"What?… I don't understand…"

"Is that all your stuff?"

"Yes." I put down my bag and attaché.

"I should probably warn you, Antonio's having one of those days." Jezebel looks toward the mezzanine, ostensibly my new room. "When he paints, he can be unbearable sometimes."

"I'll consider myself warned. What does he paint?"

"We can go take a look, if you want."

Her smile convinces me. I follow her upstairs. A man is there, back to us, talking to himself, gesticulating, shrugging his shoulders, scratching his head. "Fuck!" Every two words: "Fuck!" He turns around. He's fat, hard-eyed, unhealthy, and fearsome.

"Another one, Jezebel? Fucking hell, he won't be

sleeping up here, I hope."

"Antonio, this is Julio."

"H-hi," I say, caught off-guard by his rudeness.

He begins to walk circles around me, studying me. I have no idea what's going on.

"Do you paint, *carajo*?"

"No," I respond.

"So then why the hell are you interested in sleeping in a room full of canvases?"

I don't know, I shrug.

"Goddammit, Jezebel, I told you to find someone who understands painting, *carajo*. Okay, Julián—"

"Ju-Julio. It's Julio."

"Tell me what you see."

"What?"

Jezebel leans up against a wall.

"What do you see here?"

He means the painting he's working on.

"You can't think this long! Art hits you and that's it!"

"I see," I say, "I see a bunch of… tiny little men running around. In no order. They seem lost. Everything happens at the same time. Everything chaos."

"Everything is what?"

"…chaos?"

"So nothing makes any fucking sense?"

"I… yes. Yes."

Jezebel squints, a piece of curly hair falling across

her eyes.

He stares at the painting anew. "Say whatever comes to mind. Don't think, *carajo*."

I see I'm being tested and formulate my answers accordingly.

"A blind man sees."

"Another one. Fast."

"If you believe you don't know... if you know you don't believe."

I stand there. I have no idea what I just said. Just stuff I made up.

He scratches his chin, considering. For the first time he smiles, though it's a disconcerting and unfriendly look for him.

"Okay, Julián. Not *too* bad. Accepted. If nothing else, I like that you obey when commanded. The only thing to know around here is not to touch these canvases, because otherwise I'll break your neck." He turns and the easel is again his only concern. "Leave me alone now, *carajo*. Both of you. Back downstairs."

In the kitchen, Jezebel makes us some tea.

"So?" she asks me.

"So what?"

"Still want to stay?"

"I seem to have passed the test."

"Antonio's a crazy asshole, but he's also a good guy. If that makes sense. Before I forget, Abel will be back tonight."

"Abel?"

"You forgot? The other roommate who travels for work. He's hardly ever here, but he's interesting, too. A bit all over the place, but interesting."

I try to see through her, to judge who she is or where she comes from. Even when inviting, her eyes betray nothing. Without being cold she's distant; without being warm she's comforting.

"What are you looking at?"

"Sorry?"

"The way you're looking at me."

I have no response.

"It's not good to be so inquisitive. Even if only with your eyes."

"Sorry."

"How's the tea?"

"Good."

I drum my fingers on the table.

"Silence makes you anxious, huh?"

"And you no?"

"No."

"No?"

"No."

Jezebel gathers the empty cups. She washes them in the sink with careful, pious compulsion. There's a trace of sadness permanently clouding her look. She's hypnotic, all her person engaged in the task. I'm lost in her, as if she only just now appeared before me. She sees me wide eyed, smiles, tender and melancholic. Everything she manifests has two faces.

I like this house. It all feels necessary. The irascible artist upstairs, Jezebel and her transcendent resignation. None of it's realistic, an attribute I always associated with common sense. But that's exactly it—common, ordinary, boring. Civilization needs endless slogans and decorum to make us do what makes common sense. This place, on the other hand, makes its own sense.

By nightfall I'm more familiar with things. Jezebel, reading a Fitzgerald novel in a wicker chair in the court-yard, is in her own world. The plaster of the patio wall is cracked, bare brick bleeding through. Above, the window leading into the studio hangs open, reflecting the wavering light of candles. In the living room the walls are a sponge-painted mustard yellow standing in sharp contrast with a scarlet red ceiling. The fur-niture is eclectic, none of it matching. A picturesque oak table is circled discordantly by cheap aluminum chairs. There are two small sofas, one black suede, the other purple with white flower patterning. A stack of Antonio's paintings are leaned against the wall, the little men wearing hats scattered around their little houses with puffing chimneys. I take a seat on the purple sofa but feel ill at ease, so I get up and try the other one. I hear a meow. A big white and gray cat slinks out from underneath. It licks my hand before retiring into the closet to cuddle up between a porcelain Geisha and a tuskless ebony elephant. The door leading to the other room has been turned into a mural of scores of little men hauling buildings, bridges, factories, and cars on their shoulders before falling off into the void. I can't help getting up to go run my hand across it.

"No, *mierda*." Antonio appears behind me out of nowhere. "Don't touch the paintings."

"So-sorry."

"Stop stuttering, Julián. *Mierda, che, mierda.* What did I say? Don't touch the paintings."

He turns and disappears. I'm alone again, staring at the mural. I still want to touch it but I hold back. There really is something special here. It's the first time I've ever wanted to touch a painting.

Sometime around nine Jezebel walks past me in a blue silk dress with a black pearl necklace and matching earrings. Her legs are slender, contoured, ankles thin and white. She looks at me. "*Chau*, Julio."

I want to ask where she's going dressed so beautiful, but I can't be an interrogative newcomer. She glides out the door. Her perfume lingers. I close my eyes and allow it to affect me.

"Not a good idea, Julián." Again, Antonio seems to appear out of nowhere.

"It's Ju-Julio."

"Stop stammering, *che*." He goes back to work, cursing under his breath.

I moved in three or four days ago, maybe five. Tough to keep track. Everything here moves at its own pace, a rhythm totally disconnected from what's on the other side of these walls. I don't know how to explain it. Here I feel like I levitate without ever advancing in any normal way. In the afternoons I drink tea with Jezebel in the garden, at the small table with wrought-iron legs and checkered tile surface. At home she wears bohemian clothes. Hoop earrings frame her face in circular symmetry. Her bare shoulders, wan as a moon, are sometimes offset by an orange or yellow scarf. Many of her blouses have ruffles edging the neck and sleeves, making her look like a Port Royal *bucanero*. The jasmine flowers on the patio wrap her in an aroma that becomes embodied in her hands as they follow the flow of words from her lips.

Today I'm yet to see her, though I can hear her somewhere in the house humming old songs. In her voice, they sound new. Normally she's under the garden's white pergola, reading Fitzgerald for hours alone.

Antonio mostly paints at night, preferring to work by candlelight. When he's working, I have to remove myself to the landing of the spiral stairs. I don't go downstairs to sleep partly because the sofas aren't long enough to stretch out on, but mostly due to my own stubbornness. The light is too dim to interrupt my sleep, but when he gets stuck, when what he has in mind doesn't come or he fails to capture it, he explodes into violent tantrums, incoherent curses. He throws the brushes and the paint and punches the air. Then it's impossible to sleep. Sometimes he deems to ask me something, and on those occasions I simply look at him blank-faced, substituting gestures for words.

Despite my attraction to the place, it hasn't come without its discomforts. More than once I've considered something else, something less chaotic. My sleep was disrupted bad enough one night to prompt me to inquire about the price of a few places on Calle Independencia. All were nice normal apartments without a hint of mystery. But how can I possibly leave Jezebel and Antonio behind me at this point? If I leave now, I'll never get the opportunity again. The truth is, I'm already addicted to their chaos. The things they do I agree with in an oblique, general way. Even when Antonio cajoles and mistreats me, I don't find myself disgruntled. I see it as a consequence of his art, the seriousness with which he takes it. Maybe I just don't know how to stick up for myself; but I don't think so. Their impulses are my own, in an odd way.

Jezebel is singing, soft and lilting, about someone named Mary Carmichael, someone who faced down a tragedy like Euripedes might have wrote. I look at the kitchen clock and notice it doesn't work. A beautiful, useless thing, the wood bearing an antique white patina, thin black numerals seared into its face and two copper hands radiating from the center of a smiling sun. There are footsteps.

"Did you have lunch already?" Jezebel asks.

"Huh?"

"Have you eaten?"

"What time is it?"

"Does that matter?"

"That clock…"

"It's beautiful, isn't it? Antonio brought it back from Zacatecas in México."

"It doesn't work."

She sits at the table and looks at me, eyes still. "Does beauty need to have a utilitarian side for you?"

"I want to say it's noon…"

"Don't you see the shadows getting longer in the garden?"

"Well, usually to figure it out I would look at my watch."

"You just looked at one."

"Yeah, one that doesn't work."

"Everything has its limitations."

I make two slices of buttered bread, pour some orange juice.

"You came back really late last night," I mention.

"I come back late every night, Julio. The point is, I come back. A lot of people go home and never come back."

I nod though I don't know what she's getting at, eating the bread.

"Are you settling in okay?"

"In all honesty," I say, pausing over my glass of juice, "I don't know yet."

The sound of snoring and coughing suddenly comes from the attic.

"That's Abel," she tells me, seeing my confusion.

"When did he show up? I've been here all day."

"He came back early this morning. You two slept about three feet from each other."

"That's impossible. I never saw him."

"Maybe you didn't look."

"Where's he back from?"

"Choele Choel†."

"So I guess I have to share the room with him."

"Yeah, but he won't stay long. Idleness kills him."

"Oh?"

"Actually there were four people up there."

"What do you mean?"

---

† A town in the province of Río Negro.

"Antonio was painting a nude."

I gulp the juice.

"Claudia comes to pose once in a while. She works around the Rosedal. She's trans."

"What?"

"What I just said; are you deaf?"

"So you're saying while me and this stranger were sleeping, Antonio was painting a naked woman?"

"Is there something wrong with that?"

"I mean… yeah. Yeah, there's something wrong with it." I stand up from the table, confused.

Jezebel's eyes sparkle with roguishness.

"Do you have something against transexuals, Julio?"

"No!"

"Why so worked up then? Or maybe you have some fantasy…"

"Jezebel, what are you talking about? My problem is someone was posing naked in my room while I was sleeping and nobody told me or even asked permission. That's not right."

"What isn't?"

The snoring gets even louder. Abel coughs.

"And what about Abel? He has no opinion about all these people being in his room?"

"He's dead," she says flatly.

"Huh?"

"Ask him yourself."

"Ask a dead man if he's dead?"

"Yes."

I scratch my head. "A dead man who snores?"

"Doesn't mean he isn't dead."

"I'm going for a walk."

"Ask him yourself if he has a problem with people in his room."

I turn on my way out the door, angry, disbelieving. "Ask the dead man snoring upstairs?"

"Yeah, him upstairs."

Outside it's the ever-repeating scene. Diesel exhaust from the bus. A woman steps on a loose sidewalk tile, gets splashed with water, curses her luck and trudges on. A guy with pomaded hair leans against a wall, watches people go by. The nearby bakery feeds the air with the scent of bread. Everything as always. A guy sucks at parallel parking, can't get it right, hits the bumpers in front and behind, won't accept the truth. The newsstand crowded, and in the window of the bar across the street the melancholy-eyed old men are playing dominoes. Repetition collapses time, it's in everything and every-one all at once. I cross Avenida Belgrano[†] and think, not

---

[†] Manuel Belgrano, one of the founding fathers of the nation, fought in the Argentine Wars of Independence against Spain. Having received payment for his service during the war, he donated the money to be used by the government to construct schools. The government never used the money for its intended purpose, and it was never returned to him. He died in poverty.

for the first time, about how the government still owes this man a lot of money. Belgrano, in Rosario, before his army, holding the flag, reciting his pledge. I pause at the intersection. Belgrano as a street, as an ideal, as a hero, a man betrayed and poor. And the cross-street—unappreciated in the shadow of Belgrano's five-lane thoroughfare—Calle Perú. The death mines of Perú, result of conquest. Túpac Amaru[‡] quartered for claiming what was rightfully his. I'm sweating and I reach out for the light pole, caught up in some sort of panic attack. An obese man, panting as he crosses, shakes his head at the sight of me. I close my eyes against the faces. What if each corner were an Aleph? Where all history, all that was and will be, exists concealed? An intersection is a well-defined point, at least in the city. I regain my composure just as the light changes to green, so I walk. I arrive at Diagonal Norte. Roque Saenz Peña[§] is there, face still stone, humorless, and covered with bird shit. Calle Florida is a constant gush of people. I stop at the closest café. Jezebel told me to ask the dead. Sometimes the dead speak without you having to ask. But what if people pass through the intersection without caring to hear? Or could it be we're finally deaf?

[‡] Leader of an Incan rebellion against the Spanish in the late 18th century. He was executed, along with his family, in 1781.

[§] Former president of Argentina. Served 1910-1914.

III

Last night I slept with one eye open, worried about what happened with Claudia and Antonio. I don't trust he wouldn't include me as part of one of his paintings if the thought occurred to him. With Abel I've yet to exchange a single word. The Corpse, as Jezebel calls him, disappeared just as he came, unnoticed. I heard him snoring during the night. Finally I fell asleep from sheer exhaustion. By the time I woke up he was already gone, in his place only rolled-up blankets and a pillow with an impression from his head.

I wander around downstairs. I should take a shower and get dressed, but this apartment, universe of infinite layers, has only begun to reveal itself. I never thought, or perhaps didn't consider the possibility, that a place could take such a hold over one of its inhabitants. The pension, in comparison, bored me to death, apart from the crazy lady on the fifth floor who would erupt into endless tirades against the government. Her principal complaint—which as far as I could tell was made loudly and on a regular basis to no one at all—was that they had removed the old streetcars from the city, leaving Buenos Aires like a Venice without boats.

There was never an encounter with one of those larger-than-life people like out of a Jack London novel. Some irresistible, attention-grabbing, stirring soul. In that pension everything was all in tune, predictable, never out of place. But here everything surprises me anew each morning, like a child unaccustomed to grown-up freedoms, my notion of things uncorrupted by any real knowledge.

On the door of the fridge are twenty or so pictures of Jezebel with different men, people of varying class and style, smiling, cuddling, kissing, crying, their reactions either so discordant with their appearance as to be confusing or so completely in line with it as to provoke contempt, some maybe in the process of getting naked or maybe in the process of getting dressed.

Towards the bottom of the freezer door there's a note: *To have value the flower must grow in the desert.* Grow in the desert. My eyes hover on the words. I head back up to the mezzanine. I can't seem to go in and out of my own room without feeling like an intruder. There's a new painting set up on an easel, one I haven't seen yet. He's left it facing away from where I sleep the last couple of days. I decide to take a peek. It's the nude of Claudia. She's centered on the canvas and surrounded by multitudes of little men attempting to peek at her, study her, admire her. I'm overcome by a voyeurism that mirrors that of the little men, craning their necks from the windows of small buildings, a priest with head stuck through a stained glass window depicting Saint Paul, a police officer snapping a photo while handcuffs dangle limp from his other hand.

A sound behind me makes me jump.

"Don't be scared, Julián."

"It's Julio."

"I know, I know. What are you looking for?"

"What? Nothing. It's my room."

"Only occasionally."

"I'm the one renting it."

"True." He at least assents to this.

"This is a good painting," I admit to him.

He's looking well-rested, standing with hands in his pockets. "Claudia's fucking sexy, no?"

I'm a little surprised he says this, if only because it's a halfway normal conversation starter.

"You're so innocent, Julián."

"My name's Julio."

"Of course. From the way you're looking at her, I could've painted you, too."

"Huh?"

"You're practically in the painting already anyway."

I step away from the canvas and accidentally knock over some brushes and a pot of water.

"Nervous?" Antonio lights a cigarette. "Come on, *pibe*†, let's have some coffee."

I follow him to the kitchen. I go to the cupboard and put two cups on the table. Antonio looks at me, then the cups.

"You're missing one, Julián."

"It's *Julio*, Antonio. My name is Julio!"

"Okay, *pibe*, I know. Come on and grab one more."

"But it's just the two of us."

"Precisely. Three cups for two people. It's logic."

"I don't get you."

"So then why are you wasting time trying to understand? There's a bag of butter croissants on the counter. Jezebel brings them sometimes when she gets home late."

"How many do you want?"

He doesn't respond, appearing lost in thought.

"Should I bring *three* croissants, Antonio?"

"Huh?…three? Look at you chasing your tail. Why would you bring three if there's only two of us?"

I hang my head, bring two croissants to the table.

"What's this?"

---

† Term of endearment, especially towards a younger person.

"Two croissants. One for each."

He laughs, shaking his head.

"One, *pibe*! Just one! If there's two of us you bring one. Do I have to explain everything to you or what?"

At this point, I'm considering telling him to go to hell. I want to, but I don't. He's so sure of himself. If he's losing it, he seems to be doing it with incredible conviction.

He picks the croissant off the plate. I watch baffled as he holds it in front of him, studies it from multiple angles, then carefully, purposefully tears it in two and offers me half. He takes a bite and breathes deep.

"I'm going to see Claudita in a bit," he informs me, chewing.

"From the painting."

He nods. "We're going to take a walk."

"Just the two of you?"

"No, the three of us."

He's decided I'll be going, apparently.

"Grab something. It's a bit chilly."

"No… I don't think I can. Not today."

"Don't give me excuses, Julián. Just go grab a sweater."

He shakes a cigarette from a rumpled pack and lights it. His chest swells and he's caught all of a sudden in a coughing fit. He laughs through the wheezing.

"And Abel?" I ask.

"What about him?"

"He doesn't ever stay long?"

"Only when he'd rather be dead."

I wait for him to round the statement out. But no, that's all. He picks a hair off his tongue and finishes the coffee.

"I'll go get a sweater."

"Just one?"

"Well I'm not bringing two, am I?"

Antonio shrugs and puffs the cigarette. "Maybe I'll paint a nude of you, Julián."

I tense up.

"Nudes frighten you, I see."

"I should feel different, according to you?"

"Your emotions are yours."

"Hey. Listen to me, *viejo*[†]. My name is Julio, understand? *Julio*." I feel my eyes catch fire.

He says with unprovoked simplicity, "You're what I would call a one-dimensional man."

"What's that supposed to mean?"

"I can't just sit here and explain things to you all day. Come on."

The street is colder than usual. Not the temperature, just my feelings. Something inside feels frozen, twisted,

---

[†] In this case, the meaning is closest to "old man". But it can also be a term of endearment towards an older person, or something more analogous to simply addressing someone as "man" in English.

petrified like the Arrayanes[‡]. *Maybe I'll paint a nude of you*, he said, now walking alongside me with an indecipherable smile. Is he just a cluster of contradictions or someone who does nothing but laugh at everything and everyone? I can't help but wonder about him and Claudia.

"Antonio…?"

His look stings me to the core. "If you're going to ask me something about my relationship with Claudita," incredibly knowing exactly what I was thinking, "don't. Your mind clearly can't deal with it."

"I'm not a child."

"No, but what you're thinking almost qualifies you as one."

I break stride, throw my hands into the air in total frustration. What can I even fucking say?

"Let's go," he says, walking ahead. "Claudia doesn't wait."

I don't want to keep following. But I do. Why, I don't know. I just do.

The sidewalk stands empty. No one between us and our destination.

There's a stab of pain in my stomach.

"You okay?"

"My stomach."

"Nausea," says Antonio, looking up at the sky, cynical

---

‡ Petrified forest in the Argentinian Patagonia.

smile spreading across his face.

"It just hurts. I don't feel sick."

"Have it your way, *querido*[†] Julián. We'll have things one way and one way only."

I give up—I'm Julián. There's no point. I should leave him here, leave him walking alone on this sad stupid sidewalk, but if I don't it's because I feel I need his approval. In all things I fall short. I can't do a single thing right. What does he expect of me? He's blatantly changing answers to questions just to trip me up. But even if that's the case, it's also true he seems to know I fall short in my own eyes. I do the wrong things despite knowing I should do the right ones. I make efforts to change but then get scared of my own actions. So is his perception of me really that flawed? Maybe I deserve a bit of abuse. So I don't care what he calls me or if he wants to paint me naked. Go ahead. I have no problem with it. What I need is for this pain to go away. I need relief. I spit on the pavement.

"Hard to swallow?"

"Just a little phlegm."

He laughs.

"You always laugh to yourself, *viejo*?"

"Only when I feel sorry for someone."

He moves toward a heap of debris piled next to a building under construction. Sifting through it, he

---

† Meaning "dear" or "my dear".

picks up certain items, feels them. He feels them as if he were feeling the skin of a woman, bringing them to his cheeks, smelling them, closing his eyes. "This, Julián," he says. "This I can use." He hefts a huge chunk of rubble up onto his shoulder and starts walking like an ice man from the 1930s.

"You're going to make that into something?"

"Use for the useless." He grunts under the weight.

I watch him, smiling with genuine pleasure, carry the huge piece of concrete and plaster. His gait starts to sway like he's about to crumble. I run to help.

"Leave me the fuck alone!" His face is red, straining. "Can't you see what I'm doing here? It's my *Vía Crucis*."

We walk this way for several minutes, turning here or there, but he can never walk more than two hundred meters without stopping. He gasps and sweats. His knee drops to the ground, hand on the sidewalk, drenched in sweat.

"The first fall," he says.

He gets up, staggers wildly for a second, balances and starts again.

I can't help but try to put an end to this. "Let me help you."

His eyes are swollen and burning. In those cynical smiles, the insufferable demands, I see the obverse of an enormous sorrow, recycling pain in an enclosed loop, enough pain (and ego)—apparently—to give him a

Christ complex. We pass Parque Lezama, turn into an alley, then another, and come upon a small plaza. A stooped old lady spots us.

"That's shameful of you, *joven*[†]," she says to me. "Why don't you help him with that?"

"God bless you, ma'am," Antonio whimpers.

The lady *tsks* my laziness and walks away.

My head is exploding—I already offered to help him twice! But people believe what they see and that's it.

What she said makes me feel guilty all the same. I *am* someone who helps, or when asked at least. Antonio again falls to one knee.

"This shit is killing me, *che*."

I extend my arms and ease the weight of it on his shoulder.

"Let go, goddammit!"

I have no clue how to communicate with this man.

"You're dying, *che*. Look at you. Let me help."

"Put another hand on it and I swear to God, Julián, I'll cut your balls off."

Fucking christ. Now I really do almost leave him there, but again, again I keep following him. My stomach's still killing me.

"You have no clue how pretty she is, Julián…" he huffs. "Claudita… her skin's velvet. Eyes… she's a *dis-covery*. Fuck, this weighs a ton…"

---

† Meaning "young man".

We head down a narrow passage and come out onto a treeless street of cracked tiles and concrete.

"Come on, if we don't hurry we'll miss her. She wears these cute little transparent panties. Her beauty's revealing."

"Revealing of what?"

"You persist… in understanding nothing…"

Why am I walking around town next this human hieroglyph? I don't get these people. The Corpse, who sleeps and vanishes, the woman who entreats me to chat with the dead, and this man who paints naked, beautiful transexuals in my room while I sleep. This man who drags me along with him while he collects pieces of trash. What am I doing here? Is this what was going on all those years while I sat in front of a computer screen with a necktie and a latte?

"Are we close?" I ask.

He stops. "Impossible to know, *pibe*."

"What?"

"Are you deaf or something?"

"We've been walking forever. I imagine we're close?"

"We're always close."

"Are we going to Claudita's house, or are we meeting her somewhere else?"

"Neither."

He keeps carrying that huge piece of plaster and concrete. He can barely stand and still we keep walking nowhere.

"So then how are we going to find her?"

"It doesn't work like that. If we find her, we find her. If not…" He shrugs. "You know, we live in a maze, Julián. First a road invites you to lose yourself. Then, as soon as you're lost, all you want is to find something you know. Have you ever been to Parque Chas†?" He starts to walk again but finally it's too much and the rubble falls, cracking in two. "There it is," he exclaims happily. "Done! I'm taking this smaller piece. Let's head back, *che*."

"Back where?"

"Home."

"What about Claudita?"

"So you really want to meet her, eh? Maybe one of these nights I'll wake you up."

I shake my head, so confused I'm not even angry anymore.

"I'm telling you, Julián, her ass is perfect. Even better, she's a flirt. You're going to love her. But today it's no use. I don't see her anywhere."

"So you never know where to find her?"

"Anything that's worth anything you can't find. She shows up when she feels like it. Anyway, let's go. I have work to do. I don't have all day to waste like you." Now again with the smile I hate, the one that taunts.

---

† A famously difficult area of Buenos Aires to navigate. A common joke goes something like, "Everything you ever lost in life is in Parque Chas."

So after all that we just go back. I have the image of a half-naked Claudia wandering Buenos Aires—marble skin, soft red cheeks, feline-smooth gait and darting gaze—she takes shape in my head, but blurred, looking for a ladder which might lead her out of this filthy labyrinth.

"I saw you see her, Julián…"

We walk in silence. I feel Claudita's presence in every corner and shadow, the way Antonio's presence pervades, carrying his piece of broken plaster. The two are almost one and the same, one generating the other and together generating one.

Rather than chilly, it's hot, practically torrid. All exudes moisture. People walk by in bad moods, faces red and puffy. Clothes stick to bodies. Handkerchiefs wipe sweat from faces. We keep heading back. Antonio's eyes dart around. That face—his face—I've seen it somewhere. Those exact expressions, the same slightly distended eyes. It's him in his paintings. The little men dispersed throughout his works are him, like a quantum leap onto canvas. Within a rectangular prison, he finds his freedom, sensations becoming gigantic, encompassing a universe where he unleashes any mad instinct. That's the reason for his laugh. He sees me on the other side of the bars, living in total freedom like a prisoner.

The endless sweating has glued my pants to my knees and they keep sliding down my waist. Claudia. I want to meet her. But as Antonio said, she's a discovery. Some discoveries hide in plain sight. They hide in garbage bins, passed out against stained walls or beneath benches. They appear or disappear as they please. I saw before, I don't know how long ago, a painting of a ghostly face revolving around an obelisk built atop chaotic waves of immigration and conquest, dishes and silverware with no traces of food. A desperate civilization growing despite its own hunger, generating an ideal or a possibility.

A sudden wrenching in my stomach leaves me doubled over.

"You gonna puke, *che*?"

"I feel like I can't breathe…" Spit pools in my mouth. Antonio slaps my back and a dense piece of hot yellow-green vomit hits the ground.

"That shit kills you, Julián…"

"I have no idea what that was."

"Let's go."

How is it he radiates a sense of invincibility, of doubtless forward movement, acting in contradiction to the world around him as if he's found the secret to all things. Does he never stop to question himself? I pad along after him, little dog on a leash.

Finally we arrive back home. He gives me a pat on the back, lights a cigarette.

"All right, Julián, stay down here now. Understand?

Don't go upstairs. *Chau*."

He disappears up into the mezzanine. He may have found infinite freedom in his prison, but there seems to be room in his cell for only one. Does his egomania make him believe he's God up there, or just middle management?

The front door opens. There's the sound of keys hitting the table by the entrance.

"I'm done…" Jezebel, back against the door, sinks to the ground. Her hair's a jagged mess and her left eye is a violent blot of mascara and blood. Her shoulders are bruised. Horrified, I rush to her, put my arms around her.

"Let go of me!" she screams. "I've had enough!"

"What happened to you?"

"Nothing, Julio. Nothing ever happens. You should move out."

"I just want to help, Jezebel! What *happened?*"

She lets out an insane laugh, blows her nose directly into her own hand, clear snot slipping through her fingers.

"Who hit you? Don't tell me someone raped—"

"Shut up! For God's sake shut up and leave me alone! I need to get ready for work."

"Work? You can't go to work like this…"

"Like this?" she mocks. "Same as always, don't you think?"

I try to hug her, but she shudders and pushes me again. I want to help but I don't understand. She goes upstairs out of sight.

"Antonio!" she screams, voice trebling as if on the verge of a psychotic episode.

"Hello, beautiful… Come in here, please… And you, Julián!"—he calls down to me—"stay downstairs. Don't come up here."

I crumble to the ground. The nausea rises back through me, burns me, burns me whole. Am I the crazy one?

I hear Antonio start to cry at the sight of her. There are the sounds of him setting up an easel, readying his paints. What are they doing? She's begun to cry also. I sit in the kitchen alone. I can't take it just sitting there so I make coffee like a robot, stirring and stirring it with a spoon until an intense black whirlpool forms in the cup, my vision stuck in the vortex. I can still see her face, beaten and laughing.

"Christ, Jezebel… what a beautiful little destroyed creature you are…"

Antonio's smoke-ragged voice, full of this perverse flattery, makes my fist hit the table. The spoon flies off the saucer and a stain black as tar spreads across the white tablecloth. Vomit rises in me, burns my throat. Vomit of unheard-of taste, unspeakable color. A puddle of it forms around my feet. I can't help but cry. I want to go up there, into the mezzanine.

Their crying continues, but slowly I notice the sound of moaning. Soon, more moaning than crying. I'm numb. I have no idea what I'm doing. I head toward the stairs but stop again when the moans become unfamiliar, guttural, primitive. I pause, working up the nerve to go into my own room—*my* own room! The room *I'm* renting. I have every right, I tell myself. But I proceed slowly. There's the sound of them on the floor. Blood, there's blood on the bannister. I'm just far enough up that I can see the half-finished painting in the dim light—a naked woman against a red background being eaten by dozens of tiny men. I reach the landing and finally I see them on the floor. They're struggling, both bleeding. She digs her nails into his back over and over, bites him on the ear and there's blood.

"Is this how they fuck you, Jezebel?"

"Worse," she gasps, straining. "And better."

They're an infernal surrealism, a two-headed nightmare devouring itself. Antonio's a disgusting flabby bag of a man; Jezebel a perfect woman, nothing left over, nothing missing. A union of ugliness and beauty that's shocking, frightening, exciting. I can't see more. I have to get out.

I leave and head for Paseo Colón, taking the first *bondi*[†] to the Rosedal[‡]. I pass the greenery and stat-

---

† Collective bus.
‡ A park where prostitutes congregate.

ues of men whose names I couldn't give half a damn about right now. The sun goes down. The shadows of the buildings of Libertador grow larger. I head in the direction of the Buenos Aires Lawn Tennis Club. There are a few prostitutes on the street. I go up to a blonde and ask how much, but it's way too expensive. Moving on, a redhead stops me near one of the statues.

"Five thousand," she says.

I look at her.

"Five thousand. No lower."

"Three thousand."

"Four."

"Thirty-five hundred."

She leads me beneath the arches of the railroad tracks and unzips my fly. A minute or so in, I think of Jezebel and a tear rolls down my cheek. What am I doing? I push the redhead away.

She wipes her mouth. "I'm not giving your money back."

"Let go of me, please."

"Your type is all the same." Her eyes cut into me.

"I'm just gonna go."

"Your loss, daddy. Go run off to church."

Her voice… her voice is not female.

"I hope you didn't give me anything," she says, fixing her skirt, "fucking dirty-ass…"

I run, fly unzipped, dick flying between my legs. I go

into a pizzeria and rush to the restroom. I start washing myself madly in the sink. A customer walks in, sees me, immediately rushes back out.

A dream, just a dream. I tell myself this. I take a deep breath and walk to San Telmo. The streetlights come on and wash the dirty sidewalks in silvery glow. Everything takes on a different aspect. Groups of kids wander aimlessly. In cafes people are chatting and drinking. I fit in nowhere, not out here and not back at the apartment. I'm part of this insane wheel that spins without moving—part of it all and still alone. My body nothing more than a toy. Everything is a colossal absurdity.

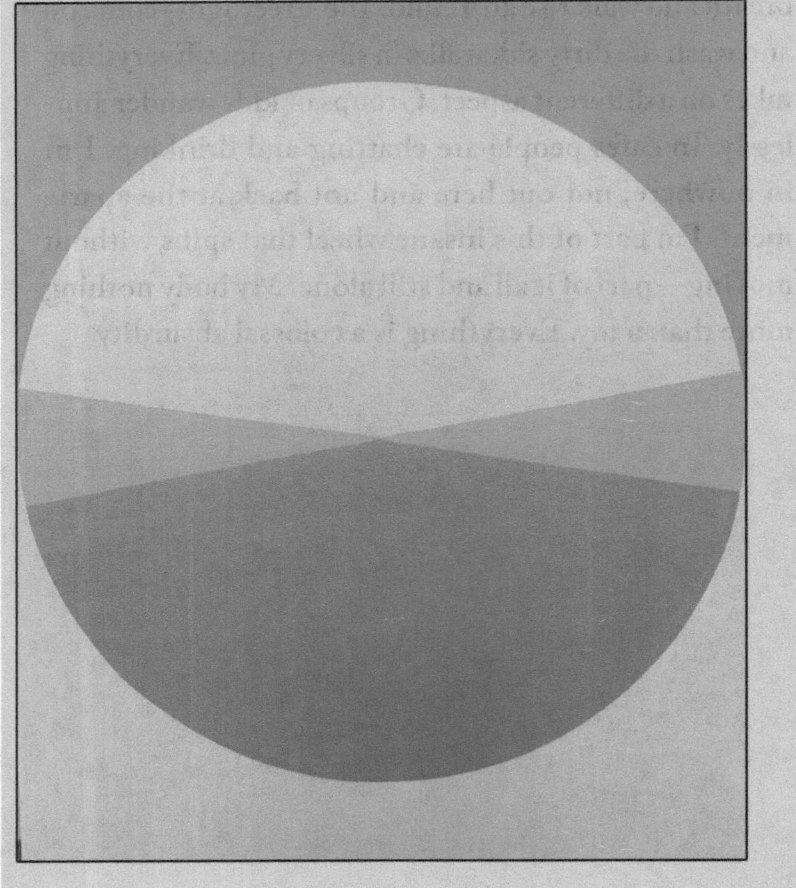

IV

The man with glasses is not happy. His brow furrows tighter with each line read. He purses his lips, wipes his forehead, shakes his head. Rubs his eyes between two fingers.

"Look, Mr. Von Artens," he says through an enormous sigh, "you came recommended by Dr. Cuellar, of Cuellar & Cuellar, so I honestly hired you without a second thought, but this report on our finances…"

"Yes…?"

"Well, I'm not sure exactly how to define it. *Incomprehensible* would be the politest word I might use. Forgive me, but it seems you've wasted our time."

"I put a lot of effort into that."

"Are you—? Mr. Von Artens, how do you suggest I explain this to the board?"

"I don't understand."

The man removes his glasses. "Well that's just it, Mr. Von Artens, is you clearly don't understand anything at all. This is twenty pages of gibberish."

"The graphics are tricolor…"

"Really? Is that so?"

"Yes, yes, they're red, blue and yellow. I used a lot of ink."

He stares at me. Wants to speak, but his lips don't move, only his eyes.

"If you want I can use four colors."

"Enough! Does this look like a crafts class in elementary school? You're an idiot!"

He rants and gestures. I don't listen anymore. I don't want to. Nothing makes sense. I don't care at all about whatever it is he's so upset over. What is all this in the life of a person? What is the life of a person in the life of the universe? And then what does the universe matter, anyway? I spend my time conducting tasks useless as human arrogance. He tosses a folder on the table. He's sweating. He rolls up his sleeves, leans toward me, face reddening and the veins in his neck bulging like bellows. He yells at me. What will become of all this in two hundred years? I get up to leave but he grabs me by the arm.

"The money… the commission I paid you… you're going to give it back right now!"

I hear something. I don't care. This guy is desperate.

He won't let go. I push him aside. He looks at me, but my eyes are indifferent and cold. He gives up. I open the door to leave and my last glance is of an ordinary man drowning in trivial problems that mean nothing to me.

V

The Corpse arrived the night before last and still hasn't gotten up. I'm eager to meet him, equal parts curious and anxious as to what I might find. I stand looking at him asleep on the floor and it's true he looks dead. He doesn't move, not even his chest with the sound of his snoring. I don't understand—how is this real? A seed of paranoia extends into a thick leafy branch. Is it possible they bring a dead person up here as a way of messing with me? I can't seem to fully put it past them. There's even a slight odor of death. Or maybe he's dead and they keep him here but it has nothing to do with me. I've heard those sorts of unbelievable stories on the news, people who live for years with the corpse of a loved one, unable to let go. I don't think I really believe either of those theories, but what does it say they even spring to mind? What other explanation is there? I try to put my bedding away but chills run down my back, as if I were actually in the presence of death. I abandon the task and hurry downstairs. At the bottom Jezebel's watching me, amused, eyes screened by dancing cigarette smoke.

"Did Abel scare you?" she asks.

I glance at the mezzanine, back to her. "Tell me the truth. Is he alive or not?"

"Nope," she says, taking another drag. Her lips are deep red. "Not at the moment, anyway. Want some coffee?"

"Stop playing games, Jezebel, and just answer the question, please!"

"For God's sake, Julio, if you're so worried about it go upstairs and wake him up."

But I can't. I don't know why. I let them get to me with all this talk of Abel being dead and ended up spooking myself. Or maybe—and I'd rather not admit this—maybe I don't want to test their sincerity. Either way, Abel stays where he is.

"I'll just let him sleep."

She laughs. "Some coffee, then?"

"Sure."

Still smiling, she moves towards me and deposits her lips on mine. There's the brush of her tongue, her hands, her nearness. She pulls her head back. I assume this has something to do with the other day, when she came home bloody? Maybe some belated feeling because I tried to help her? I lean in to embrace her, but she pushes me away.

"No, Julio. Tenderness isn't passion."

Per usual, I've started another day in complete confusion. I sit in the kitchen with her, drinking my coffee and not thinking. Next to me, she smokes and runs her fingers through my hair. Images click through my head—her flying through the door with a bloody eye and bruised flesh, her and Antonio rolling on the floor together, her nails digging into his back and drawing blood—faster and faster until I can't deal with it anymore. I'm ashamed of everything. My own excitement, my inability to act on it, my sudden fear of Abel...

So I leave; I thank her for the coffee and get out of there.

I walk Avenida Independencia to Calle Defensa and from there towards Plaza de Mayo. On Calle Florida I mingle amid the office workers, opportunists, tourists, pickpockets, and beggars. Different worlds weave together, intertwine, get a glimpse of one another, touch even, but do not mix. A small Romanian girl stares hungry at a bank of hot croissants outside Confitería Richmond while a man at the window seat feasts on one, biting into the warm flakiness while staring at his phone. Only a window between them, but the glass is an impassable border. A group of Japanese tourists poses for a photo in the Galerías Pacifico while a pick-pocket lifts the wallet from the purse of a secretary stepping onto the bus to take her back to Lugano. All one big harmonious mess, though the harmony is just a trick of the mind that allows us to carry on through it all with a semblance of order. Assigning sequence to things keeps us insulated from what is otherwise chaos. Perhaps that's a nice apologia for numerology. Passing a newsstand I scan a headline announcing the disappearance of a seven-year-old girl from a Portuguese beach while here we all just go on with our lives. We read these things, but it makes no real difference. People lament tragedy one second and then perpetuate it the next. Like right here, this blonde lady draped in a fur coat cringing at the sight of the poor old woman pulling a cart full of soda cans. I used to see the world a certain way; I can't anymore. I don't even see it the same as I did two weeks ago. Bit by bit I'm falling away from all that. How deep can I fall? And is it possible to stop myself? I lean against the cool marble of a corner shop, batteries, umbrellas, handbags arrayed in the window. Nausea again, the same senseless burning. I cough and spit. People swerve away from me. The world sways. Across the street is the bookstore El Ateneo. I enter the repurposed theater house and take a seat in the café. Here I am, anchored, nailed down into this world that straggles back and forth with corroded soles and blistered feet, groping in the unknowable for reason and baring fangs at the irrational. These are the kinds of thoughts that made it impossible for me to continue on with Susana. I couldn't share them with her; or, rather, I could have, but under no circumstances could I have expected her to take them seriously. She was too deeply ensconced in her own numerology. For a long time I considered that a practical habit, a habit which kept what felt like a whole series of competing selves at bay. I could, for instance, sit here and conceive of myself as an unemployed financier, as I recognize myself, the thing which marks me as successful, unsuccessful, failure, limited, etc. But just as easily I could see myself as nothing more than a man, a human being, sitting here in this place amongst readers and coffee drinkers, an empty symbol that could be literally anything at all. In yet another sense, my value in this place is as a customer, someone who pays for something, a living transaction stepping about a shop owner's proscenium. It's an easy and constant thing to dehumanize oneself, just a matter of obedience really. Every interaction constrained by some label. Even the coffee in front of me, waiting for me to drink it, waiting to be consumed, to be converted into something else, conceives of itself as something, a transaction or a chemical spark. But if I don't drink it, it grows cold, it sits and waits to be cleared from the table by the waiter, taken away somewhere else, a disappeared little girl off a Portuguese beach. This is all something I remember from readings of Sartre back in my university days. He was one of those writers who students read on their own time, capable of stirring up questions in adolescents and pulling the curtain back on the whole production, so to speak. Though a typically predetermined favorite, I remember being quite angry with him. Is the purpose of philosophy to sicken or cure? Why should an intelligent man wish to call everything into question, and then those questions into question, until you sit somewhere asking who and what you are: accountant, customer, coffee drinker, final resting place of the contents of my cup—what the fuck? Me, my cells, rearranged according to the roles I play. We are all people in the abstract only. Surrealist works of accident and creation, full of imperfections; a joke that's nothing other than a manifestation of the whole. One's being is a matter of indifference to existence. I disappear; another one no different replaces me.

A group of teenagers stampedes aisle to aisle and a trio of old men limp past titles. The security guard on his break calmly sips a cortado, still in costume but out of character. No one is what they really are. It's sad. It's sad how we built these lies up over thousands of years and now our essence is finally buried. Why were we in such a rush to leave ourselves interred under all this?

I pay the check and leave, moving between people on

the street. In every woman, I see Jezebel. I see her naked on the floor with running mascara, spitting bitter litanies in broken voice. I hear her wallowing with Antonio. I hear Abel's dead-man snore.

Tomorrow I've got a small job at a bakery owned by a friend of mine. I promised I'd help him with payroll, balance the books. I head home, a moment of hesitation gripping me before I enter. Once inside, though, there's seemingly no one, no noise, no lights. Up in the mezzanine, Abel remains asleep. I go to the kitchen. When I turn on the light, there's a naked man sitting at the table.

"Turn that off, goddammit!" squinting against the sudden brightness.

"Antonio…?"

"I said turn it off!"

I reach for the switch and the room goes dark again. "What the hell are you doing naked and in the dark?"

"What do you think I'm doing? I'm living. Living as designed."

"Naked?"

"Well maybe *you* came out of your mother's womb in a little dress, but I happend to come out like this."

He stands up, walks to the cupboard and retrieves a mug. "Come sit, I made coffee."

I do as he says. He sits down at the table and his breasts fall flabby against his hairy chest. He's an unpleasant sight.

"Enough staring. I know I'm a monument to eroticism, but…"

I look off towards somewhere far away.

"You're not comfortable with me like this? Maybe if I put on some shorts, right?"

"I mean—"

"Not a chance! I won't give you the pleasure, *carajo*. Look at me for what I am."

"Okay. And what are you?"

"What do you mean what am I? I'm a fat man in my fifties decaying day by day. I've never been any kind of beautiful creature. In short, qualities are not distributed equally. Ergo, equality amongst all is a democratic myth. We go panting after what we can't obtain in any way." He leans back imperiously and lights a cigarette. "Did you see The Corpse?"

"Huh?"

"He died again. Just a little while ago."

"I don't get what you or Jezebel are talking about with this guy. Who is he?"

"Why do you have to act so dense, Julián? You know what I'm talking about."

I don't bother defending myself. He gets up again and goes to the counter, testicles moving unflatteringly between his thighs, and returns with croissants. He scratches his stomach and the skin reddens.

"Nausea again?"

"With you like that? Sure."

"Life made me this way, Julián. What reason do I have to hide?"

"Well, do you go outside that way?"

"Of course not."

"So then why here?"

"In here there isn't the same illusion as exists out there."

"And what illusion is that?"

"For starters, freedom, rights, and civilization. Then, if you skip through the middle, you arrive finally at your own existence."

I steer him elsewhere. "Have you been painting?"

"No. Reading."

"Anything worthwhile?"

"The story of Hipólito Bouchard."

"I know that name. It's a street, right?"

"Yes. My great-great-grandfather knew him well."

"Mm."

"He was a corsair in Bouchard's crew."

"How did that come about?"

"It's a long story."

I look at my untouched coffee. "I have time, I guess."

He stretches in his chair, back arched, right hand scratching his scrotum, puffing away on a rapidly shortening cigarette. His torso folds with fat once again as he returns to a comfortable position, holding for a moment of silence as snoring emanates from the loft.

"Hipólito Bouchard," he says, "was an extraordinary figure. An adventurer, professional French revolutionary, captain, corsair, and disillusioned defector. He played a role in the Argentine Revolution and then finally, finally *viejo*, he became Supreme Commander of the Peruvian Navy. He also happened to be uncommonly ill-tempered."

For a second I regret encouraging him. I seem to have knowingly given license to a windbag. On the other hand, though, if he's busy telling some grand story there's no need for me to speak, no real need for him to play a bunch of mind games with me. And, surprisingly, as I settle into my chair and drink my coffee, Antonio's uncompromising spirit, channeled in all its fullness into the story, becomes, after a minute or two, magnetic, even a bit comforting.

"By 1811, Julián, shit was piling up fast for our poor little infant Republic. Wars flowering all about, fueled by traitors, opportunists, power-seekers, fortune-seekers, and everything in between. The Spanish were trying to drag us back into their empire. The navy, under Bautista Azopardo, had been destroyed in San Nicolás. The Spanish got their hands on our Maltese admiral and clapped him up in chains. He spent the better part of ten years in sunless dungeons as sanitary as one of

Victor Hugo's sewers. They were also besieging Buenos Aires from the Eastern Bank, which would eventually become Uruguay."

"From Uru—?"

"*Callate*†, Julián. I already know everything you're bound to ask. Yes, Uruguay, the Eastern Bank. The Spanish, assisted by a faction of royalist Uruguayans, tried to take the city using the Río de la Plata in 1811. Some of our neighbors helped fill our fine air with fire and cannonballs. So it was shit on top of shit. The government, patriotic as they might have been, were about as organized as a bad cabaret. Each played their role, but the show was just chaos in low light. My Tata, my great-great-grandfather, worked as a boy on a ranch outside Belgrano. But his dream, *viejo*, was to set out to sea like Melville's Ishmael. That was what he told us. His name was Manuel, but we called him Tata. There aren't men like him anymore, *che*. I won't bother sidetracking us to heap curses on our own sad era..."

He clears his throat and stabs his cigarette in the ashtray.

"So because the government had no navy, they were forced to issue letters of marque. The issuance of such licenses was common. The English used them a lot. It worked like this—the government would grant individuals permission to attack, seize, loot, or destroy

---

† Meaning "be quiet" or "shut up".

any vessel bearing an enemy standard. The spoils were divided between the state and the licensed privateer. Understand? They were contracting out pirates. Corsairs. The United Provinces of the Río de la Plata issued trunkfuls of those goddamn letters to the Americans, mostly Marylanders. The government granting the license would provide ships and kit, provisions and personnel—people taken out of jails or kidnapped off the street or rousted out of poorhouses. Drunks and criminals and dreamers. So just imagine: many of these mercenary expeditions went to complete hell. Whole crews would perish. People got shipwrecked, stranded, and generally met their end in all sorts of ways. When that happened, they were exempted from reimbursement. If an enemy ship was boarded, the corsair was required to hoist their sponsor's flag. Funny, no? An undeclared war. Just a brawl between families, if you like. Guillermo Brown, for instance, was a privateer. So was David Jewitt, who took the Malvinas. So that's how it was, Julián. An Irishman created our navy and a Yankee gave us those islands. Romantic times, *viejo*. Idealistic times, no matter what you might think of them. But here's the point. A guy named André-Louis was a Frenchman from Bournes, who had adventure in his blood. He left home after his stepfather squandered his inheritance. He enlisted. He followed Napoleon to Egypt, then into the bloodbath of Santo Domingo. But what he missed at the end of these excursions was the purity, the freedom of revolution. The original fucking *core* of the thing, *che*. He'd had it with Napoleon, with the politics and hypocrisy. He was an anti-monarchy radical. So in 1809 he changed his name to Hipólito Bouchard and sailed off to the Río de la Plata and fell in with Mariano Moreno's faction, putting his naval experience to use for the Primera Junta. This was how he found himself involved in the ill-fated expedition to San Nicolás, where, as I said, the Argentine navy fell to the Spanish. After the defeat, the government put Hipólito on trial for cowardice, but he was acquitted when it was proven his crew had deserted him in the heat of battle. My Tata, still just a young man living at home, had come to idolize Bouchard by that time. Not just as a hero of the nation, but as a symbol of what he longed for, which was adventure, danger, glory, *carajo*, my Tata dreamt of glory.

"Bouchard continued fighting in revolutionary campaigns for a few years, but in 1815 he met Anastasio Echevarría, a prominent lawyer and the secretary of the National Assembly, who went on to finance Bouchard's letter of marque for the next several years. He was given two ships, one of which my Tata enlisted with as a sailor. Finally he would follow his dream, under the command of the legendary captain. Their destination was the Pacific theater, and Bouchard set sail for Cape Horn.

Tata was aboard the second ship, under Bouchard's second-in-command Oliverio Russell. On Tata's maiden voyage, there in Cape Horn, he was shipwrecked by an enormous swell and Russell perished. Tata survived and was absorbed into the crew of Hipólito's remaining ship. The crew, along with my Tata, devastated by the early loss of their first ship and suffering a crisis of nerve, attempted a mutiny when Bouchard refused to reverse course. This was my Tata's introduction to the sea.

"Despite the crew's discontent, they pressed on. The situation brightened when they happened to come across Guillermo Brown's tiny fleet. The temperaments of Brown and Bouchard were opposed. Brown was cerebral, calculating, cold. Bouchard was hot-blooded, audacious, and irascible. Through some divine recognition, the two acknowledged each other's brilliance, and it was decided that they should join forces and attack no less than the Spanish fortress of El Callao, one of the largest strongholds in all South America. I used the word 'fleet' before, but the reality was they had only three small ships between the two of them. These were madmen, *che*. So what can I tell you? They did as they said they would and attacked the fortress. This time my Tata would get his first taste of glory. Against all odds they overtook the royalists and sank several Spanish galleons. They captured one as well, a ship named *La Consecuencia*.

"They continued on as far as Guayaquil, where they staged another attack. This time they fell short of glory. The offensive failed, and Guillermo Brown fell into Spanish hands. Hipólito, faced with the capture of such a prominent Argentine admiral, couldn't escape the failure of the venture, and offered the enemy the entire spoils of the campaign against El Callao for Brown's release.

"But it wasn't the end of their attacks against the Spanish. They sailed on, continuing to commandeer and loot until Bouchard's ship, ragged from its narrow escape from the squall in Cape Horn and a lifetime's worth of cannon fire, lost its seaworthiness. At that moment Brown made the decision to once again separate their two forces, though not before gifting his unlikely friend-in-arms *La Consecuencia*. Grateful, Hipólito took the vessel and rechristened her *La Argentina*. He was also given a second ship, which he gave to the same officers who had attempted to mutiny against him, and they parted ways. Why would he do that? Come to your own conclusions, but my interpretation is it was a clear matter of honor amongst thieves."

Antonio, after three cups of coffee, is up again making more, continuing the story, voice laced with caffeine near to the point of shaking, living out his words to their conclusion.

"That was just my Tata's first expedition with

Bouchard. The second came a year later, again financed by Echevarría, this time east to Africa. The crew, newly assembled, was composed of British and Creole sailors. Before they were even able to embark, a massive brawl broke out between the two. The only thing that was finally able to stop it was a contingent of naval marines. With this harmonious group, *viejo*, Hipólito and my Tata were again seabound upon *La Argentina*. They crossed the Atlantic and docked in Madagascar in just over two months' time. But the way there was turbulent. The differences between the crew that had led to the brawl in port flared up once again at sea. The Creoles, who weren't used to maritime discipline, clashed often with the British, sailors *par excellence* who carried the profession in their genes. In the course of one of the fights, someone set a fire onboard. The crew managed to contain it, but at the cost of a grave wound to my Tata. The incident left him with a massive scar that ran across the entirety of his shoulder and chest.

"In the port of Tamatave, Bouchard ran across a British commander seeking assistance in enforcing the crown's laws against slave trafficking. Working together, Bouchard boarded several slave ships docked there while the Englishman detained them with his ship's cannon. According to a law observed by the British called the Right of Visit, which gave them royal authorization to board and inspect foreign vessels for contraband, Hipólito relieved the slavers of both their human contraband and, as payment for services, their loot. So outlaws also perform heroic deeds, Julián. At least if the price is right.

"From there, *La Argentina* headed east in search of bounties. They skipped across Java, intending to pass through Asian seas. In doing so they encountered their own kind. A group of Malayan pirates intercepted them, and a violent skirmish took place. Whether out of skill or luck, Bouchard once again emerged the victor. They massacred the Malayans and absorbed one of their ships into their fleet.

"Next they attempted to blockade Manila, a territory of the Spanish crown at the time. They sank more than a dozen ships, looted twice as many, and took hundreds of Spanish prisoners.

"They sailed to China. I'm unclear what happened on that leg of the journey, but by then Hipólito had taken a liking to my Tata. More than once they shared the bridge together, as well as the spyglass. I believe the Frenchman liked him not just for his bravery and because he was a fellow adventurer, but because of what he represented. Bouchard must have seen in him, Julián, as I still do sometimes, the candid hope of a new country, a new ideal and a new identity. A new promise to the future.

"In 1818 they docked in Hawai'i, called at that time

by the English the Sandwich Islands. They were well-received by King Kamehameha, who was so moved by that motley and savagely romantic fleet of Argentine pirates he became the first sovereign to recognize the independence of the United Provinces of the Río de la Plata. *La Argentina*, just as many crews before them, lost themselves in that tropical paradise of uninhibited women and a people uninterested in war or jealousy. It was an open secret Tata fell in love on that trip, but he never mentioned the woman's name. There's a possibility he never even knew. It was a love he enjoyed rather than possessed.

"Somehow they left there for yet more adventure, though I'm sure it wasn't easy. Soon they sighted the California coast and the massive Spanish fort off the coast of Monterrey. This fleet of madmen, on their own, were going to attack one of the bastions of the Spanish empire in North America. Their attack met with bad luck, Julián. As they approached the fort, the wind gave out and they were stranded in full range of the guns of the fortress. They were pummeled with cannonballs. Not sunk, but defeated in less than ten minutes. They were left to float immobilized off the coast in humiliation. This might have been the end of them. But Bouchard knew that the Spanish, after the rout, would be celebrating the victory deep into the night. The soldiers got hopelessly drunk, and at dawn on

November 24th, with nothing but a few small boats to bring his men to shore, Bouchard conquered Monterrey and raised the flag of Argentina."

"The Argentinean flag on the coast of California?"

"Yes. And I'll tell you something else. Tata was the one to hoist her up. He said tears fell from him like a baby. And in a way, Julián, that's what they were in those days. They were a country in diapers, dreaming naively of an empire."

"So then what?"

"They manned the fort for five days, waiting for a Spanish counterattack that never materialized. They got bored. No women, no food, no adventure. So they looted the surrounding towns. Then they got bored of that, too. So they sailed far south to San Juan Capistrano and looted that. Then they kept going. They reached Central America. They attacked San Blas, then Acapulco. Then Realejo in Nicaragua. Because they were a country in diapers, and that means more than just the romance and the ideal. Children in diapers play with things for a while and then forget them, not knowing what to do and shitting wherever they feel like.

"And just like children, they eventually got in over their heads. The fate of *La Argentina* wasn't to return to Buenos Aires bathed in glory, but rather to be commandeered by a Chilean admiral. Bouchard was arrested, brought to Chile, and charged with being a Spanish mercenary, if you can believe that. While he defended himself in court, *La Argentina* was left unguarded in the port of Valparaíso and the ship was looted. Everything they'd gained in their campaigns. Everything! All of it stolen and never recovered. La Argentina was destroyed and sold off as firewood. Not by coincidence, Bouchard was cleared of any wrongdoing not long afterwards. He left prison and reunited with his crew only to find it had all come to naught.

"But they still weren't done, *viejo*. Bouchard, accompanied by my Tata, enlisted with San Martín in the campaign to liberate Perú. The effort, as we know, was successful, and ultimately Hipólito was named Commander of the Peruvian Navy. It was the cause that drove them, not this or that flag, or the geography of some certain place."

Antonio sips his coffee, staring at the table.

"So what happened to Bouchard?"

"After that Bouchard spent his life in solitude on his farm in Perú. Remember I said he was ill-tempered? He could be a cruel man. He met his end at the hands of his own servants, a group of whom stabbed him to death in 1837. I actually find this to be a glorious end for him. He died the way he lived. Anyway, it took 120 years for his remains to be brought back to Argentina. They stuck the guy there in the Pantheon of Buenos Aires. So that's it."

"And your Tata?"

Antonio sighs, puts the coffee down. "Poor old man… He had a lot of dreams, a lot of exploits. But I'll tell you, Julián, that in reality he was deeply marked by everything he'd seen and done. He claimed to hear voices in his head that never stopped screaming. Not shouting, *screaming*, in pain. He killed for his cause, and eventually got killed. He was a loyal guy, really loyal. He fell during La Revuelta del Callao, defending the new Peruvian government. And Bouchard, of course. His captain."

We sit in silence a second. "You talk about him like you knew him. But if he died that long ago…"

He looks at me, face placid. This is the first time we've had a conversation where he didn't swear constantly, wasn't condescending. Called me *viejo*, even. I have no idea if the affection is for me or for the people in the story. Why is it I always feel like some disappointing child seeking his approval?

"I know it probably seems to you like I'm exaggerating," he says, "but my Tata kept a diary. His wife, my great-great-grandmother, passed it down, hand to hand, one generation to the next, and eventually it ended up as mine. In a sense, I did know him."

VI

Jezebel is more beautiful than ever, eyes shining under the dark cloak of night. It's a chilly November evening. I look at her. She's unaware of my presence. I've been hidden here almost fifteen minutes, just around the corner, contemplating her. I know I should tell her I'm here—I'm practically right next to her. But no, tonight I'm the French gendarme in the Marquesas watching the island women bathe naked in the lagoons. In short, I'm the invading admirer. I lean my head against the wall in shame, the shame of a boy caught up in his first love. My head is as clear of Hipólito Bouchard as the day I was born; life is now a constant, horrific exaltation. Everything inside me goes a million miles per hour: heart, lungs, head. I can't remember the last time I melted so completely over a woman. When you get to a certain age you think it's not possible anymore, but here I am hiding from her, old enough to make a sad voyeur of myself and enjoy my own suffering. She turns and her eyes impale me, glowing with moonlight, infinite alterations of looks and blinks and moods. The jasmines are in bloom, she and their fragrance melding into dizzy poetry. Her hands lace across the coffee cup, the lines of her fingers standing out surreal and impossible. She sits on the patio in the breeze, hair dancing mildly, taunting my infatuation.

She turns startled. "Julio?"

"Hi," I say, too fast. "I just… I just came down and it's a beautiful night…"

She looks up to the sky. "Very beautiful. And the tea is nice and warm. Take a seat."

She pours me a cup.

"Here. It's Egyptian chamomile. Antonio's up there painting, so it's pointless to be inside. But it looks perfect out here tonight. Someone wrote once, 'Today I can write the saddest verses…'"

"Neruda," I nod, looking at the floor, away from her brilliance. "From The Captain's Verses. *Il poeta d'l poppolo.*"

"Abel just left."

"The dead man."

"No," she corrects, "the living one." Taking a sip of tea, her wrist is a fleeting sculpture.

"Not seen many hands in your life?"

"What?"

I'm forgetting I'm not hidden anymore.

"Some people look each other in the eyes when they talk."

I try to relax. "Sorry."

"I doubt you'll be getting to sleep early tonight. Antonio's going insane. Whenever you hear loud music then you know he's in there painting naked and won't stop till late. Plus, it's Liszt."

I smile, not honestly giving half a damn about Antonio.

"What do you think of Liszt?" she asks me.

"I'm not familiar with his music."

"Are you embarrassed or something, Julio? You can't look me in the eyes?"

I find the courage to look at her and say it directly. "They're too beautiful."

She laughs. Something between irritated and dismissive. "Next time we talk I'll put on a veil."

But she accepts the compliment, doesn't spurn it entirely, and it's enough for me. Her out here on the patio makes perfect sense. I feel less out of sorts for the first time in a while today, finally remembering I'm not a little boy.

In the space behind her something odd takes shape… a clock… something. Someone takes note of something… a man with glasses. I see faces… I don't understand.

"Hey, wake up, *che*. You in there?"

I close and open my eyes. There are no more faces. Just Jezebel looking at me.

"Abel told me he said hi to you the other day."

"He did?"

"He said you didn't even acknowledge him. You were lying on your back with your eyes open, but you were in a trance or something."

"Me…?"

She nods.

"I don't remember." Someone with glasses taking notes. I rub my eyes.

"Tired?"

"No. I should be, but no."

"Well, you won't see him for a week or two. He left for Bolívar this morning."

The volume of the music up in the mezzanine rises quickly, twice. Antonio turning the dial. Liszt resounds in San Telmo as he never did in Europe. Antonio's voice cuts through the orchestra. "There! Red, *carajo*! Red like your fucking pain!"

Jezebel and I look at each other, crack a smile.

"I told you he's going insane," she says. "Someone called him from Tokyo today to talk about organizing a show."

"Seriously? Tokyo?"

"He's sought after. He's got a name."

On cue, his voice returns. "And blue can send all this shit to the bottom of the ocean! God*dammit!*"

We can't help but laugh. I laugh like I haven't in a long time, until tears form at the edges of my eyes. But still—and it bugs me—the face with the glasses won't leave me alone.

"Jezebel?" I ask, "can you look over there for me? Behind you? Do you see a face with glasses?"

She laughs again, thinking I'm playing some game. "You're just trying to get me to turn around."

"No, seriously. Can you look?"

Her smile dissolves. She looks where I ask her to. She turns back and meets my eyes.

"The one with the glasses?"

"Yes. *Yes*. You saw it?"

"Don't pay too much attention to them, Julio. They come and go. One day they're here, the next no one finds them. They're ghosts. More tea?"

I push the cup away from me, breathing deep.

"Want to go for a walk?" she suggests.

Again, Antonio from the attic: "Black as nothing!"

"Christ," she says, rolling her eyes. "He's driving me crazy. Come on."

Out on the street we can see his shadow in the upstairs window, pacing about to the sounds of shouting and violins. Maybe Jezebel was right. I can't find the man with glasses anymore. Maybe he was never there in the first place, or was a vestige of something that was and is no longer.

The cobblestones gleam tired obsidian. We enter the dark mouth of Calle Chile, façades of decrepit mansions slumped like corpses. Jezebel explodes against the blackness of the street—a star reflected in a puddle of pitch.

Amazingly, we can still hear Antonio's epithets echoing through the neighborhood.

Buenos Aires is lit to its finest, lights defying the night, inviting people to leave their hovels, go for a walk. At some other latitude, in some other world, everyone is inside watching TV. Jezebel's grace highlights my awkwardness. We turn at Avenida Belgrano, heading for Paseo Colón. We can see the newest portion of Buenos Aires, built in Puerto Madero. Tempting in its sheer opulence, we resist going there. Tonight, we know who we are. We're a pair of bohemians, and the city that belongs to us is a different one altogether, the one transposed beneath the high rises, the one of small passageways and uneven streets. Mansions and tenements. The city born in the port, carved into the shore by wave after wave of immigrants.

"You like to walk?" Jezebel asks, observing the distant towers.

"Sometimes."

"Tonight?"

"Tonight I love to walk."

"Let's have a cortado."

We go into a French-style café with wood floors and tables the color of brown shoe polish. Our luck holds and there's a free table right by one of the big arched windows. The lights of the cars passing outside alternate red and white.

"Can you believe what we built in these ravines, Julio?"

"What did we build?"

She looks at me like Antonio for a moment—like I'm an idiot. "Buenos Aires," she says. "You don't ever think of the things sacrificed to build this place? All the despots and madmen who contributed? Here, we let the lunatics free and keep the sane locked up. It's so beautiful I find it offensive sometimes."

How she describes the city is how I would describe her. She speaks like she owns it, is in full charge of its paradoxes and policies.

"Our cemeteries invite the living. We expand and contract how we want, build and destroy and always succeed despite ourselves. The description Borges gave was best. He said Buenos Aires always existed." She stops, looking into her cup. "Anyway, I don't see myself anywhere else."

"You're feeling philosophical tonight."

"Whenever I have a day off, melancholy hits me all

at once."

"So you're not working tonight, then?"

"No."

"You always work at night?"

"Sometimes."

"Doing what?"

She looks at me, eyes brimming with accusatory sadness. She leans over and kisses my cheek.

"I love walking around Buenos Aires on nights like this. I feel clean and innocent. The streets never disappoint."

"At our age things in the city still surprise you?"

"The capacity for wonder grows with age. Come with me," she says, grabbing me by the arm, barely leaving me time to bring my cup along. She leads me to the bartop. There are two open stools to either side of a man in his late fifties. He's grayhaired, a bit bald, wearing a beige suit with patches on the elbows and tortoiseshell glasses. Jezebel pushes me onto one of the seats. She takes the other.

Taken suddenly out of his solitude, he greets us in a low voice. He's drinking gin. Arrayed in front of him are six empty measures. Jezebel signals the bartender and buys us all a round. Limoncello for her, gin for me and our new friend.

He takes the shot without even waiting to say *salud*. He sets the glass in front of him and now there are seven.

"I have a piece of advice for you two," he slurs, rubbing his eyes so his glasses go up to his forehead and blowing his nose with a distressed handkerchief. He wipes his fingers on the sleeve of Jezebel's blouse. I almost yell at him for this but she allows him to do it, looking upon him with tender eyes.

"Don't ever mess with justice," he says. "She isn't blind. She's—" stifles a hiccup "—she's one-eyed."

"Why's that?" Jezebel asks.

He raises a finger, leaning it one way then the other. "She eyes whichever side suits her." Smiling at his own wisdom, he puts the same finger further up in the air to order his eighth. "It starts as a game," he says, voice gravelly with age and liquor. "I meet her at the San Telmo fair. Carlita. Carlita is a… a… a *beautiful* woman with black hair… green eyes. She comes to my stall looking for Castillo on vinyl. Sure, I have them. I sell her three. Now she comes back a week later and buys two little German dolls, some trinkets from the 1920s. She comes back every week for three weeks or so until one day I refuse to charge her. I give her a silver *mate* glass. I shouldn't do it," he says, downing the shot put before him and eyeing Jezebel, "but here you go. But I don't think twice about it because she invites me to dinner. Carlita lives in Villa Urquiza, on Calle Bucarelli. I bring over two bottles of wine and a frozen dessert. And we spend the night talking, talking of everything, until the morning is turning bright again, and when we're done talking about everything a man and woman can, we speak with our bodies."

He starts to cry in his glass, his ninth. He continues with tears down his cheeks and voice blubbering. I'm embarrassed, but Jezebel keeps her eyes on him. She will hear any confession, will endure any number of tears.

"And Carla comes to the stalls on Sundays to help me. She knows how to sell antiques. She can sell anything to the Americans. Anything more than forty years old is an antique for them. But the toughest are the Turks because they understand this business well. They're not fooled by a smiling Argentine. With her, the business is getting better and better. We go live in a house on Calle Chile, a few blocks from the plaza. She… she suggests I open another shop in Bolívar, between Calle Estados Unidos and Carlos Calvo. I always wanted to, so I do it. I invest everything I have… *everything*… I stock it with antiques from all over the world. At first we both take care of it. But she says let's split the days. I'll work Monday to Thursday; she'll work Friday to Sunday. That way we can still take care of the stall in San Telmo. She wants more free time to search for product, improve our shop's reputation. Now it's *our* shop. She hasn't invested a single cent, but I believe it's ours. I add her name." His eyes track the words of an invisible sign. "*Lázaro y Carlita Antiques.*"

"Lázaro," Jezebel says. "I bought something once at your store. A Chinese vase. But…"

"…but you didn't see me there?"

"No."

He goes on and on. We both know how it will end, but it expands and contracts like Jezebel's Buenos Aires, time an elastic band. He can't seem to end his story. Jezebel listens with the patience of a saint. I'm not so holy and urge her off her stool. We leave him there, drowning in gin, Carlita ever in the process of conquering his life and his business. Finally I convince her to leave. She kisses the drunk old man on the cheek the same way she did to me twenty minutes ago and prepays another gin. As we're leaving, I hear him starting all over, rehashing the same sequence of events. We step back out into the night.

"See, Julio?" she says.

"Absurd," I say, "but surprising. Borges would approve. A labyrinth of stories."

"You understand, then."

We go through Plaza de Mayo and turn onto Florida. Beneath the marquees, hidden from the lights above, are the beggars, self-arranged at even distances from one another. A girl of ten years old—eyes dull, dry lips deeply scored—approaches and extends her hand. She doesn't speak; only with her eyes. Slumped down against the wall in the shadows is her mother. We neither give her money nor stop, and once we're a few meters away she curses us. Jezebel bites her lower lip but says nothing. From Santa Fe we enter Barrio Norte.

"Another cortado?"

"Sure."

At the corner of Santa Fe and Esmeralda we find ourselves swimming against a column of protesters, enroute somewhere for some reason. Never a lack of things to protest around here. We go into a shy little café between two tall buildings.

At the table, she slides low in her chair, leaning her head back. "Poor guy…"

"Who? The guy at the café?"

"He lost everything, Julio. Couldn't you see that?"

"I guess. But he was a bit of an idiot, too, don't you think? He should've been more careful, letting her take over one step at a time like that until it was too late."

"Loneliness blinds," she ripostes. "It makes you believe things that are only true in your head… it makes you hope. Hope is La Loca, it's irrational. It makes no sense but it's always there."

"Why does hope make no sense?"

"Does life end in death?"

"Yeah, but that doesn't—"

"But what? Everything is lost already, and we live in hope. We're even stupid enough to hope for the existence of some metaphysical world that will save us from the only thing we have as an utter certainty. Hope is a ridiculous weed growing out of a crack in the pavement."

I find her uncharacteristically maudlin in this diatribe, though I try to consider her words, take her seriously for whatever she means. "Maybe that's my problem," I say.

"What? Hope?"

"Lack of it."

She tilts her head. "Without hope there's no reason."

"Reason for what? I thought you just said hope is ridiculous?"

"Reason to live. Look at Breton—he chose the irrational. He chose the hope of love over his own surrealist doctrines when he could've just offed himself to prove his own point. On the one hand, it would've made good sense, but he would've been dead. There's nothing without craziness and irrationality."

I understand her point, but now it's my turn to be a bit maudlin. "But when I look, Jezebel—if you understand what I mean—when I really look at things, all I ever see is human beings used and abused in the name of production. Attach whatever connotation you want to that word, but it's the word I want to use: production and more fucking production. And then in the middle of it all, like a knot, is monotony. I don't know, maybe I'm just talking to talk, but everything is boring to me— sometimes more boring with age—and boredom isn't an enemy anyone wants. One of the greatest enemies, actually. If we're going to start dropping famous names, how about Baudelaire? Monotony was his nemesis. He chose the bottle, in the end."

In response, Jezebel leans across the table and takes my hand. Her skin is softer than velvet. This moment is certainly not boring. She looks me in the eyes and it's instantly clear why the man at the bar couldn't help but start spilling his guts as soon as he saw her.

"It must be difficult to be you, Julio," she says softly. I can't decide if she's sympathetic, sarcastic, or both.

"And nothing's difficult for you?"

"Everything. Everything but my life."

"I don't understand."

"How should I explain the unexplainable?"

"Don't we always try to do that?"

"The answer is usually in the question."

I want to kiss her. I could, easily, right now. But of course I won't. Because I always do what's expected of me, don't I? I never step out of line for even a moment. I feel her gravity; I'm a moon spinning around her, tired eyes shining on her surface, but I won't cross the distance separating us. She refuses collision. Sometimes I honestly feel like there's nothing underneath, nothing behind the veil, and maybe that's—

"Are you okay?"

"Hm...?"

"What's wrong?"

I rub my eyes.

"I just need some air, probably."

"Do you want to go?"

"No, no, just give me a quick second."

I feel suffocated. Sometimes it happens all at once, like getting bad news you're not expecting. Everything, or maybe just one thing, feels too real, to the point of being unbearable. It can start with nothing more than a thought, but then my chest tightens, pushes my lungs inward, shrinks them, and I suffocate like an asthmatic. Psychosomatically. Psychoasthmatically.

She looks concerned. "Was it something I said?"

"No, just… everything. I don't know…" A dot of white slime falls on the table.

"I don't know what to say. I'm sorry."

"It's okay." I'm bold enough to bring my hand to her face, stroke her cheek, though not bold enough to kiss her. My lungs contract as if hit by a surge of electricity. All the air is pushed out of me in a burst of violent coughing. I fold in two and fall out of my chair to the floor. She supports my head in her lap, saying something I can't hear or can't process. The table is surrounded by people. There's a doctor taking my pulse.

"As far as I can tell, there's nothing wrong with him," he tells Jezebel. "Likely it was an anxiety attack. He needs rest."

Outside, we cross at Callao and Santa Fe in stunned silence, just two more amongst the crowd, bathed in blue neon.

Two blocks down Santa Fe she finally says something. "Tell me, Julio, how long do you plan to stay at the apartment?"

"You want to kick me out or something?"

"No," she says, evading the truth probably. "Just a question."

I decide to ignore the implication and just answer how I feel. "I almost left after the first week. Everything with Antonio and the thousands of little men and being constantly wrong about everything—no one could've blamed me, I know that much. But little by little I got used to it. Maybe I'm less bored there than I normally am. I don't know when I plan to leave, or if I even want to."

"What about the lack of space? Lack of privacy?"

"Space and privacy are exactly what would terrify me at the moment."

"What about us? I'm sure you notice we prefer to be rude sometimes."

"Well…" I equivocate, trying—ridiculously—to be polite in the face of this admission, "like I say, I'm not bored."

"A person has no end. Like a barrel without bottom."

"I wonder if it has a beginning."

She stops walking before I can stop alongside her. I turn.

"And what do you think?" she asks.

I shrug. "I don't really know. Is the question so important you have to stop in the middle of the sidewalk?"

Some strange expectation in her collapses. Her mouth tightens and she starts walking again, right past me, head down.

"Hey," I say, catching up. "What? Did I disappoint you or something?"

"Yes, actually. Your lack of courage."

"Lack of—? I don't answer your silly question and so I have no courage?"

She stops again, agitated. "Courage isn't about what's around you, it's about what's inside, what you don't or can't know."

"Jezebel, this doesn't make any—"

She holds a hand up. "Don't, Julio. Let's just keep walking."

She keeps going, now as uninterested in my answer as the rest of the world. I know she's punishing me, and it's working. My goddamn fear again, fear of doing what I think I shouldn't. Fear of delving into myself. How can I know who I am if I don't know what I am?

We walk on and on. I'm just following her now, hangdog and lost. She glides through the streets, the sublime and yet utterly ordinary person she is, putting me out of her mind as easily as if I were no one to her. I can see she isn't going to stop any time soon. We retrace streets, navigate intersections packed with cars that play chicken with pedestrians, and all the way I limp after her, looking at her in amazement. She called me a coward. Why?—because I seem so superficial to her? Because I don't answer her question on command? I just had an anxiety attack, for fuck's sake. I'm a half or maybe completely lost person who just wants a little company, and this is how she treats me.

Finally I can't take it anymore. "You're too harsh, Jezebel."

"Truth isn't harsh," she says, not breaking stride, "because it knows nothing of severity or laxity. It just is. You're the one lost in adjectives."

I think to counter her on this. "So if you take all the adjectives out of life, what do you have then?"

"Everything."

"No," I say, "you have nothing left."

"Are you slow-witted or something?"

"What?"

She laughs, finally stopping and turning to face me. Across the street are two girls standing by a street sign, eyeing us curiously.

"Look at them," she says. "Does it surprise you the way they're looking at us?"

"A little, I guess."

"Describe those girls."

I breathe out and hang my head. Always another test or demand. "Fine. One's tall, with straight shoulder-length brunette hair, a little thick around the middle but good posture." I stop, not liking this.

"And the other?"

"Tall as well, a little taller than the other one. Hair is brown, coppery brown. She's cute, she's well-dressed. They seem like good friends."

Jezebel stares at me.

"What? What did I say wrong?"

"You didn't say *anything*, Julio. You just throw out a mountain of adjectives and say precisely nothing. You talked for a whole minute and have nothing to show for it."

All I can do is look at her.

"You're talking about the dead by describing the coffin."

"Jezebel, what are you getting at?"

"Think."

"I don't know how to win this game you're playing."

She sighs, looks at me with pitying disdain, apparently relinquishing her frustration with my stupidity. Again, but this time with ultimate condescension, she kisses me on the cheek.

We keep going all the way to Plaza Italia. We're still not talking. We exchange a few glances, but that's it. The remains of the Sunday fair in the plaza is a skeleton of empty stalls lined up one after another in two long rows.

"On Sundays," Jezebel says, breaking the silence, "all this explodes into life, but tonight it's just a phantom image. The stalls suggest something, tell stories of the city. Goods sold or stolen, price bidding and discounts. Don't tell me they don't speak to you."

"What, the stalls? They're just a bunch of pipes and awnings where people set up shop."

"And how do you see them?"

"Empty," I assert, both playing dumb and avoiding giving any other answer for fear of her response.

"That's it? Look at them, *carajo*." She's doing an impression of Antonio, almost…

I look at the long rows of stalls, the endless aluminum poles and wooden fronts. I try, but nothing comes to mind.

"I said what I meant, Jezebel! I see them as empty."

"You're just hiding in adjectives. Put all that to one side and just see things for what they are for once." She walks over to a stall and stands before it. "This stall, Julio. This stall is."

I wait for her to finish, but she's just standing there looking at me.

"You don't understand?"

"Okay, it *is!* Is that all you have to say? That's your grand answer?"

"That verb is deeper than all your adjectives. Everything begins in being."

Frustrated, I go and lean against one of the empty stalls. Empty, yes, *empty*, because there isn't a vendor within a fucking mile. I'm starting to get dizzy. The plaza is spinning, and the passing cars get bigger and smaller but never stop.

"You're just as crazy as Antonio. I say the stall is empty, so it's empty."

"Are the crazy people the ones who heap endless adjectives onto what they are, or those who simply are, who are content with being? Have you ever heard it said that the universe is an infinite library made up of innumerable rooms?"

"Of course. That's Borges again. What's your point?"

"The library is inhabited with every kind of person imaginable, tirelessly seeking all the answers to their questions, some who will kill each other for those answers, on and on forever. Get it now?"

"No!"

"Everyone tries to define something as good or bad, useful or useless, vindicate or ban things, but never leave them neutral."

"You've been using adjectives this entire time, Jezebel!"

"The point," she says, "is that people can do without language. What does it have to do with understanding things? Has it ever gotten *you* any closer? It's just that foolishness, that obsession, to describe what's incomprehensible by means of words that's the cause of confusion. In the story, remember?—the library is looted by those searching in vain for some book of answers, but in the end they find nothing. Here we are, in another room, and you find nothing."

"But I take it you do?"

"I'm not looking for anything, Julio. I just am."

"I wasn't looking for anything, either, but you pushed me here with all these games."

But I do think I finally understand what she means. I'm worn out. I can see the very first signs of dawn, maybe only an hour away. I don't give a shit about the stalls, whether they're empty, an infinite library, or anything in the goddamn world. All our conversation this whole time has heads nor tails. Life does sometimes feel like a huge adjective that weighs me down and prevents me from thinking, moving, acting. I just want to be happy. Is that even possible? Jezebel would tell me happy is just another empty adjective devoid of value, apart from being a description of an unattainable state.

We go on walking until the sun's up. Our silence, oppressive before, is relaxing. We walk. We live. The morning is brisk. Another adjective. The night is… what? Anyway…

VII

The days pass—do not fly by—they just pass. Move at a constant rate, perhaps a bit accelerated with respect to chronological duration. I used to be a connoisseur of duration, of the kind inhabiting expensive watches on wrists. The prison is only subtly camouflaged; people love their parameters. I seem to be yearning for those parameters today, to once again inhabit my familiar prison. Everything or nothing; who knows; it all gets cloudy around me. I get lost in the mist that settles over the landscape of my thoughts, a sailor who loses the advice of the stars and ends up stranded. I'd like to put a stop to what twists and unravels before my eyes. If it were indeed possible to freeze it all, I would study it, understand it, but its protagonists form a labyrinth to rival those of Jorge Luís. Jezebel remains a constant desire, though her duration is boundless in every direction, and so I'm consumed by desire's cancerous self-reproduction, intestines, liver, kidneys; once it passes into my bloodstream my heart explodes, but before bursting it swells, gives me the feeling of wanting to fall apart into pieces of insane happiness. She hits me like sunlight off metal. In my desolation, it seems as if Antonio owns her. He paints her. He paints her naked as easily as dressed, whole or in pieces. Like the one he finished yesterday, depicting her little finger, obsessively watched by dozens of pairs of eyes. Green, blue, honey-colored, brown, black. Less obsessed than hypnotized, hypnotized by beauty embodied in a little finger. Antonio summarizes Jezebel's beauty for me with the persuasion of an essayist and the ecstasy of a sentimentalist, located in that portion of her, his army of little men dropping down from roofs, crowding onto balconies and emerging from sewers, huge eyes on undersized bodies, all drawn toward that single radiant object. *What an achievement*, I'm helpless to think. But it's true. That bastard fucking nailed it. Exceeding beauty provokes a decoupling in the body of a human being. I hate him.

A little finger dwarfs us, me and the little men. No one can explain why that finger should be so beautiful except the whisper of instinct, a whisper that doesn't need an explanation to fill me with excruciating admiration. Before, in the parameters of my old cell, I likely wouldn't have thought twice about this painting. But now I'm floating in utter freedom, unable to move past a simple fucking little finger. My parameters just changed shape. I can't remember what my life used to be like, if a person's life can indeed be divided into a before and after. I died. I followed Antonio and Jezebel into the streets of Buenos Aires, trailing after them like some porteño Jack Kerouac after Neal Cassady and Ginsberg, going towards the light, and I died.

Today the loft is quiet. Antonio went to wander the streets in search of garbage and debris. He'll be sifting through pieces of masonry, broken bricks, twisted iron, boulders of concrete buried under mountains of sand, bits of bark… He said before leaving, with typical vaingloriousness, that he was going to "reassemble what society has disassembled." I'm falling under his influence. I don't deny it even to myself. This apartment is a cult of personality, and he's the Charismatic Leader. Jezebel is his first lieutenant. Abel… well, I would rather he go on sleeping.

With everyone gone I can imagine the loft as my own. The paintings seem mine, even. I handle the brushes, picturing myself creating some chaotic beautiful meaninglessness. Is it possible for a human being to do anything meaningless if everything in his body makes sense, even a single eyelash? Would that mean all nonsense is formulated through meaning?

Antonio's new painting is hidden under a black-and-pink-stained sheet. Whatever's underneath remains obfuscated, sacred. I remember wondering, quite some time ago, did Hölderlin succeed when he succumbed to madness? Or Rimbaud, with his syphilis, amputated leg, and endless desert? A world without sense made perfect sense for people like them. People like Antonio. Or is every seer also a liar? Do they truly hold the key, or are they just purveyors of religions, of attempts to lift the sheet? Mystics and priests stranded in vast forests are no less relatable for their desolation. They remain stuck in their attempt, like all of us.

I drop one of the brushes in a pot of water, watching the colors thread about before overtaking the liquid. I can feel Jezebel up here, the little finger wrapping around me. Inside it, I curl into the fetal position. I lose myself in there, in the cradle of soft skin. I relax and breathe. All slows down. My vision is clear. I see a wood composed of giant trees, bushes growing beneath them. I step on the head of a pope, Paul VI or maybe Pius IX, but they're just little bushes. I follow, through the wide tree trunks, a lighthouse rising out of a blue ocean. I see and follow. All makes sense just as it makes none. I breathe without hesitation.

VIII

All is again strangely quiet. No sound comes from the mezzanine despite Antonio having been entrenched up there for who knows how long. Abel arrived back home at some point while I was out and hasn't come downstairs since. I don't expect to see him. He's dead as those buried in the first graveyard and those who will be put under the ground in the last, dreaming an eternal dream. Jezebel doesn't take her eyes off her damn Fitzgerald novel. I liked Fitzgerald before; now I'd like to throw that book out the window. As with Antonio, she seems to prefer the company of the dead today.

I'm left to myself, lonely and alone. Back during my old life with Susana, I was never alone. Sometimes I desired loneliness with quiet desperation, the sheer indifference of others, the untying of every knot of responsibility. Now I have it. Antonio, Jezebel, Abel—they don't care where I'm at or what I do.

Leaned up against the hallway wall and smoking, I feel my heartbeat grow within me, becoming enormous. There, somewhere just past Jezebel in the courtyard, someone bows his head and whispers something in the ear of a woman with lines quilted around undaunted eyes, a hard straight nose, serene manners. Whatever's being said is muted by the sound of pumping blood. They look in my direction, discuss something. The woman nods. She nods again. I lean my head back against the wall, move it side to side. Well, anyway, here I am, so have a look if that's what you want. Julio or Julián, depending who you ask, wearing all blue for some reason and standing here being whatever it is I am. I don't know what that is, but I hope something. Just a person. Someone standing here and smoking alone, trying to belong. I touch the wall behind me, feel it, try to incorporate it into myself, but it's another body, separate and solid and unflinching against my presence. I pay attention to my own blinking, locked up in this body. Slowly I slide down the wall till I'm sitting, put my head between my knees, knees linked by my arms. The cigarette hovers in my fingers. Distant, unrecognizable voices.

I raise my head, study my hands front and back. Tendons, veins, arteries beneath the surface. These belong to someone. Separate them from me, put them on a canvas, and what are they? Dismembered and re-presented, like the woman reading Fitzgerald in the garden, taken apart by the man upstairs and put on display for others. What does that imply? I light another cigarette. I close my eyes and half-images flicker like old film. A bird diving through turbulent air, wings straining to keep its tiny body righted, plunging madly. The little body drops roughly past obstacles and impossible physical forces to somewhere very deep down, my mind twisting and growing small behind it, and there's just brilliant, familiar darkness, something far away, unreachable or maybe just unseeable, something which is taken away or destroyed at the very moment of birth. I don't know how, but the scent of cigarette smoke reaches down here, a faint voice calling one of my names. Julio. But what door to open? What window will return the image I wish to see?

I push myself. Deform, reform, become plasmatic. There's a burning in my fingers and I hear a distant complaint. I'm cold down here. Shouldn't it be that towards the center there would be heat, suffocating heat? I don't smell the cigarette anymore. I want to go back but don't know how. Landscapes appear. These are all just blunt, confused metaphors, but I try not to subject them to matters of taste. I am no one to judge here; here, seated and smoking, under observation. Vast ice cliffs, sun shining above them, but I am down somewhere in gloom. Climbing, I slip again and again. My hand becomes an immense fist, and it falls against the cliffside like a mace in a quarry and everything explodes. The cliff opens and I make my way. The light grows. I'm touching something. I open my eyes in the middle of a scream. I see a blurry image of Jezebel, book in hand and eyes of cruel wellbeing. I leap at her. We fall on the floor, rolling, I kiss her, she kisses me. She pushes me away, studies me. She cries, and I do too. We cry. Off in the courtyard, the angular face of a woman scribbling something, sighing, rubbing her eyes.

"Look at me, Julio," Jezebel says.

I do. I'm seated on the floor and she's standing above me. Her eyes are dry.

"Look at you. You burned your fingers. Are you on drugs? I'm warning you, I'll know if you're lying."

"Drugs?"

She leans down and yanks up one of my sleeves.

"What's this?"

"What?"

"These little red dots on your arms! Those are needle punctures!"

I look at my own arm. I cry and put my head against her. Somewhere, I hear a door close. Who closed it?

"Jezebel, I… I never…"

"Shh, Julio. You're safe with me."

"Green, *carajo*, green! Like the stupid fucking English countryside! Yes, Claudita, that's what I want!"

"Antonio?" I ask meekly. "Is he back?"

"He's been screaming up there with Claudia all night."

"What about Abel?"

"We were talking for a while, but he went back to sleep. He never stays awake too long."

I try to pull myself together, to ignore the inexplicable, but I'm lost.

"Let's take care of your fingers. Christ, the cigarette's stuck to your skin. Since when do you smoke?"

"Did you see them, Jezebel?"

"Who?"

"The ghosts…"

"Stop looking, Julio. You'll waste your life doing that."

"I just want to know who they are…"

She cleans my burn and bandages me. Only now am I starting to feel the pain.

"Give me more, Claudita! Don't pay attention to Abel, he's dead asleep! He died of love! He adores you! But never as much as me!"

How much life in that room; how much death in this body.

IX

Antonio, once again in search of trash, went out into a morning that stretches blue and fresh over Buenos Aires. I, on the other hand, woke up with a migraine. The pressure in my parietals is ungovernable—my brain is a moment away from flying everywhere in a burst of gray goo. I stir a coffee on the table before me but can't lift the cup. I grip my head with both hands and beg out loud for the pain to stop. When I open my eyes there's light… not the warm natural light of the apartment, but different… fluorescent and burning. The man with the glasses is there again, writing something in a notebook. Just as quickly his image disappears. The light and my pulsing head form a fire, consuming all realities. And yet, improbably, whether of my own will or something else altogether, blue windows form through the flames. Recognizable colors are there, bright and crisp as ever, congregating about immense butterflies unfurling velvety black wings hatched with yellow stripes. They fly off, come and go, float calmly about a thick white inert locust stuck to the surface of a leaf. I want to go there, enter through that frame, but it's smaller by the moment, the head of the locust turning toward me before taking sudden flight, getting confused with everything… the flame consumes me like a heretic and it's all gone. There's someone in the fire, in the raw light, a man with a very distinct set of glasses. He seems easily capable of writing amidst the flame. A phantom, maybe? My head drops and a huge noise shakes me. Something warm drips onto my bare knees.

"Julio!"

I'm unable to lift my head.

"Julio, what the hell is *wrong* with you?"

A white hand tipped in yellow fingernails lifts my head from the table and leans it back against the chair. A wet rag wipes my forehead.

"No… I don't have a fever…"

"I know. You split your forehead open on the table!"

"How?"

"How am I supposed to know? I heard a noise and came running. Are you trying to kill yourself?"

"No…"

"Then what's wrong?"

"I don't know, it's the migraine… it's intense…"

"Stay here. I'll be right back."

"Wait, Jezebel… don't go…"

The flames of pain return, much worse now. The man with glasses, head turning through odd vectors, reappears. No windows this time. No escape. Only pain. I groan, and it eventually grows to a shout. I can't take it. I feel my head bounce against the table again.

The same hand gathers me up. I sit, trembling.

"Stop it, Julio! Don't be an idiot!"

She cleans my forehead with something. I feel a sting. The skin there grows numb. She gives me several pills that I take with the coffee. Gradually the flames die down. I see her now. Laid out on the table is a plastic first aid box. She's preparing a needle and suture.

"So on top of everything you get migraines, too…" she says, working at the wound. I feel the punctures but not the pain.

"Eight," she says after a while.

"Hm?"

"Eight stitches."

"I didn't know you knew how to give stitches."

"I know a lot of things, *cariño*[†]."

I try to feel the cut on my head, but she stops me.

"Don't. Let it heal."

I look at her. I feel drunk, almost—woozy from the pain, vulnerable from her gentleness and care, sad from confusion.

[†] Meaning roughly "my sweet" or "my dear".

"Who are you, Jezebel? Who are you really?"

"Just what you see."

"I see a lot."

"Yeah, well, the state you're in, I'm not surprised."

"I don't see smiles on your lips. What I see are tears and sadness. I see someone beaten down."

She looks away.

"Look at me," I say, "the man with the glasses is gone…"

"What?"

"You're covered with bruises. Every time I see you in the morning, there are new ones. On your shoulders and arms. And your dress and hair and makeup are messy. Who's doing this to you?"

"Does it really matter? Anyway, you know already."

"Of course it matters. Tell me his name."

"There are so many."

"So you're in some kind of violent relationship with someone."

"Aren't we all? Who just did that to your head?"

"I did."

"So you're in a sadistic relationship with yourself, then."

"That would be masochistic…"

"I suppose that makes it better?"

True to form, she has new bruises this morning, one on her cheek even. She hasn't showered yet. Her dress is limp. Something morbid grips me, but it's something I can't control when I see her like this. A beaten woman should make me feel pity, but the sad truth is it turns me on. Her bare bruised shoulders and untidy hair; her dull, unfeeling eyes; her smeared makeup and white legs.

"Julio," she demands angrily, "stop staring!"

My eyes sink with shame.

"Everyone just wallows in the same mud, don't they? You're no different. No one's different from anyone."

"When I see you look like this in the mornings," I admit to her, eyes still on the floor, "I can't help it. It's just lust. You're right. I'm no different."

Surprisingly, I feel her hand slide onto the back of my neck. I look up and she's right in front of me, breathing slow, heavy, silent. She touches my face, but I notice her blinking too much, hesitating.

"It's a bad idea, Julio," she says, threatening me in every way possible. Threatening to kiss, threatening to pull away, threatening me with what I want.

"Suppressing everything is a better one?"

"There are consequences for everything."

"For me there aren't, unless you and Antonio…"

Her face registers surprise, but also something close to disappointment, as if whatever I said was something supremely childish.

"There's nothing else to say, then. I didn't know you and he… So he's the one who beats you."

She sighs, frustrated with me again. "It's not as simple as you'd like it to be."

These are indeed things I'm not sure if I truly want to hear, yet I can't stop bringing them up.

"The world beats me senseless."

"Antonio's just one," I say.

"Listen to me. The whole world beats me senseless."

She leans in and kisses me, now reduced to little more than a gesture of compassion. I feel, coming into contact with her, a large and broad pain, the private pain under the surface of the world, under the surface of people, the pain and ugly truth of desire. It's a momentary freedom. She moves her lips away and looks at me through half-open eyes. I grab her by the shoulders, tight, so tight she cringes with pain.

"You're hurting me!"

Frightened, I let her go. I see my fingers have left marks on her skin, alongside the others.

"The world beats me senseless," she repeats.

"I'm sorry."

She looks at me, eyes full of betrayal. "The real problem," she says, getting up from her chair, "is I've already forgiven you. We'll keep the stitches in for a week."

She leaves. Maybe it's too obvious, maybe I'm just the same as all men, but I see her as a martyr. Love is pain. She soaks it up like a sponge.

X

I wake up with another migraine and it starts all over. It's fucking impossible, but it's the truth. I looked in the mirror a while ago and my eyes were more red than white.

I'm alone up in the mezzanine, in what's supposed to be my room, but the truth is I have nothing. Every time I lie down, it's possible I might not get back up. If not from my skull imploding, then from sheer indifference or confusion. Someone is up here with me after all, it turns out. I can hear Abel snoring.

For some reason I have a flash of déjà vu, almost nostalgia, remembering a whole different era of migraines past. Then, as now, existence turned fuzzy under the weight of the pain. I remember screams, thrown chairs and shattered dishes, and most of all the diamond-edge of a perfect headache: pain, bruises, purple spots, the slow destructive march of molten earth across the terrain of my thoughts and my life. I remember my sister, too. These days I never see her anymore. With time and distance things can become unreal, people and places, things you know you did but can only be sure of if you remind yourself. I suppose the same is true with irreparable damage between two people. Anyway.

I can't even guess what day it is; I'm just here in darkness. Earlier, when the pain was only starting to come in like an ocean tide, I did my best to read Artaud, all that madness and suffering, but in the end I had to stop—I feel I might have him beat at the moment. Jezebel, you're nowhere to be seen today and I need you. Your face brings me irrational hope. Instead, I'm stranded up here with the dead man. I'm just as dead as he is today.

I don't know what time you left the apartment, but I remember Antonio painting till late morning before heading towards the door with a bunch of rolled-up canvases under his arm and an unlit cigarette stuck between his lips. He cast a quick glance at me and said, as if performing for a roomful of people, "*Che*, put one between your eyes already! Who could possibly live in that hell of yours?" Then he walked out laughing.

You won't approve because you guard Antonio's callousness the same way you guard my sickness, but I yelled as the door closed that he could go fuck himself, that I would burn every last one of his paintings to ash. I had no choice. But my head, shit, Jezebel, my head is killing me. And Abel's snoring, now that I notice it, is like a chainsaw. I'm stuck down here, a weight against my chest and red-hot spikes jamming my forehead, eyes and neck, all the way down to my groin and knees. Do you ever want to break free of your own mind, Jezebel? Do you ever wish you could get up and leave it behind you? Fly away from it, even just for a day. My damn head. Artaud had his lilies and his unpolluted skies; I have monotonous groaning complaints and tears. Where did you go? I miss the distraught makeup, your weary clothes. Your crying… I even miss your orgasms when you fuck Antonio. You know so much…

I envy you. That's the truth. I'm just a piece of fluff the wind blows around. I exist but have zero control over it. In these flashes of pain, I sometimes think I discover something about myself. I think I see the antipodes of my mind. Equidistant to my point of reason stands my other self, the one none of us knows except through the little windows of our dreams. Just glimpses. As soon as I start to really see something in its fullness, the pain finds vent and leaves me tarred flat against the ground, panting like an inmate after a beating. Tell me, are you the one who runs the prison? Antonio's the executioner, of course, but are you the one who orchestrates it all? I would like to ask Abel, but the fact is he's dead, and the one who comes and goes is always a different person.

Off in the corner I see some clothes lying on the floor.

I crawl to them. They're yours, this bloodstained shirt and bra. I smell you on them. But there's an image that appears and it's that woman, the woman who writes. I see her. She adjusts her glasses, jots her thoughts. I want to get her attention, but she can't be real. Only you are real to me.

I try to crawl back to my pillow but instead I just give in to the pain, to the snoring and the loneliness here without you.

I'll fly… fly away from everything like I wanted to. Fly over a solid mass of blue. I don't need to understand anything. Or at least I'd rather not. The thing about flying, I realize now, Jezebel, is that I see from above. Mountains of ice, jungle plateaus, savannahs and deserts. Everything extends everywhere, with no beginning or end. Hector and Achilles fighting to the death. A huge mass of men and beasts charging a tiny group at Thermopylae. In the pit of a crowded coliseum, slave souls decapitated one after another. A crucifixion stops the life of an entire region. From up here, it's always the end of the world, the end of infinite worlds, but down there no one cares, they just continue with their murders and their migraines, politics and painting, sacrifices and conquests. The Puerta del Sol reaches Tiahuanaco. In Asia the world moves forward while in Europe it self-destructs. Goya, Van Gogh, Gauguin, Modigliani, mustard gas, and gas chambers. Quinquela strikes the brush in the port of a forgotten country. The pain in my head is subsiding. Someone to my right takes notes. I'm naked. I have a bloody shirt and bra in my hands. Water falls over me and I can see more clearly. Hot water. I wash my face. How did I get here? A hand pulls the curtain aside.

"Feeling better?"

"…?"

"I found you curled up on the floor—naked and shivering."

"Huh?"

"Just telling you what I saw, don't ask me. I got you up and brought you in here to the shower." She reaches out and tests the water with her hand. "Good, it's warm now. It always takes a while. When you feel better, come down and I'll make tea."

"Wait, don't go."

She stops, eyes burdened.

"These are yours."

I hold out her clothes, soaked and dripping pink.

"Thanks," she says.

"How did I get these?"

She holds a finger to her lips. "Shhh. Just stay here in the shower for a while. You've been through enough already."

I grab my head; I break down.

"Good, Julio. Cry. Tears are redeeming."

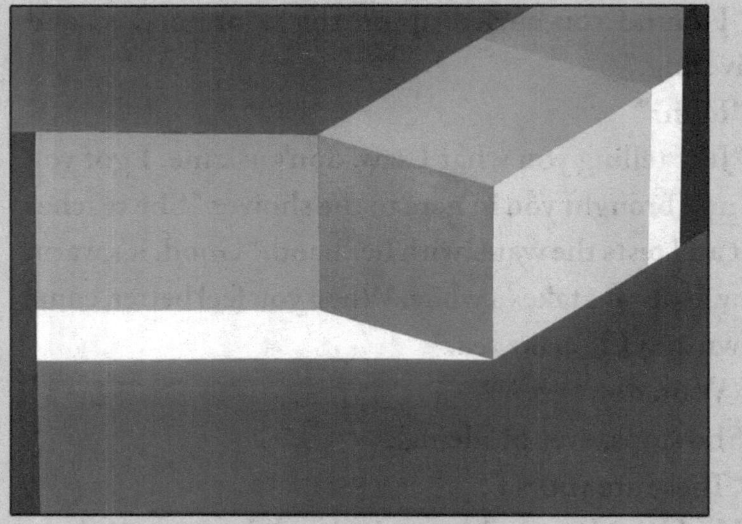

XI

After half a week of unrelenting migraines, I woke up with a mind as luminous and mild as an early autumn sky. Memories and dreams are once again organized and placed on their proper shelves. A voice in my head warns me to be wary, don't trust this return to grace, the pain will come back any moment, but my relief is impossible to deny.

The street welcomes Antonio and I, full of possibilities. His smile doesn't bother me today, doesn't strike me as the slightest bit cynical. Instead, he's been reconstructed as a monument to hope.

He lumbers under the weight of a pair of bricks balanced on his shoulder, whistling. He must be in a good mood. Every so often he flashes me a huge grin coming across a pile of rubble. Buenos Aires suits us both perfectly at the moment. With no pain, life is easy.

"These are just what I needed, Julián," he says.

"You're going to make a grill or something?"

Rather than scold me, he laughs good-naturedly. "*Sos boludo, che*†*!* Since when did I give you the impression I'm a bricklayer?"

"What else do you have?"

"Marble dust, quartz, salt, a few other things."

Crossing Paseo Colón, he stops and picks up a soda can.

"Anything and everything, huh?"

"Nothing's useless. I like to think that way, that nothing's useless. *Ni los negros del Africa*‡."

I stop in my tracks, abruptly offended, as he lumbers on. He doesn't even bother to look back.

I catch up to him. "What do you mean by that?" I ask, perhaps not strong enough to confront him directly, perhaps scared to hear what he'll say next.

"Everything I say has a political overtone," he says.

I don't find this much of an explanation. "Everything you say has a political overtone. Even when you call Claudita beautiful? Even when you say you love her?"

"Yes. But that's about inclusion as much as it is about politics."

"So to you she's just a subject for the sake of inclusion."

"Sure. Why not drag the divine through the mud a little? If I wish to include, why shouldn't I cast it in a

---

† Meaning roughly, "Don't be an idiot!"
‡ Meaning, "Not even the blacks of Africa."

political light?"

I do my best to ignore him and we continue our walk. He peels back the city, finding his treasures beneath its skin. We encounter a homeless man sitting at the edge of the sidewalk on a flattened cardboard box, thin but with an enormous unkempt beard and smelling of sweat and piss. Antonio lays down his bricks and offers the man the remainder of a pack of cigarettes and his lighter.

"Well, come over here, *che*," he says, making the man stand to retrieve them.

He does so, mutely indifferent, taking the items. But his eyes widen when Antonio throws his arms around him, embracing him. I see he's not comfortable with the contact, but Antonio has him and there's nothing he can do. Antonio exits the hug and throws a hand jovially against the man's shoulder, smiling wordlessly before turning and hefting up the bricks again.

Walking away, I feel disgusted with him all over again. I feel I know the lesson he believes he was trying to impart, the personal set of ethics he was trying to follow.

"You didn't think to give him any money?" I reproach.

"To whom?" he responds, feigning stupidity. Clearly, he has every intention of provoking me.

"Who do you think?"

"Money?" he says, twisting the word around as if it's the most incomprehensible thing anyone ever suggested in the history of known speech.

"That's the word I used, yes."

"Why should I have thought to give him money?"

"Enough!" I say, stopping again. "Do you think you're teaching me some kind of lesson here? Because if so, you're an idiot."

"Julián, has it ever crossed your tiny brain that maybe, just maybe, money is the worst thing you can give to someone in need?"

"Ah, here comes the grand lesson, the grand moralizing, from the man who jets off to Tokyo to sell images of Claudita, who he deigns to include in his little paintings, and of the woman he fucks bloody. Please, share this wisdom."

"And why do you think people buy those little paintings, *boludo*? Why do you think they pay thousands of dollars for them?"

"Because you're shameless enough to use your privilege to depict the essence of others and then cash in on it. Because you're included and they're not."

"Precisely. Finally, you find yourself capable of answering a question correctly! That's right, I'm shameless with the truth. They'll pay to fly me out to Tokyo, or Miami, or Mexico City, because they know when I get there that what they'll see is the truth, *carajo*! What I say is the truth, the expectation, and whatever's lacking in the hearts of people who view my art that they wish they could live up to."

"I've never heard so much egotistical bullshit in my life."

"Don't insult me by lowering my importance to ego. I am above ego."

This I can't even formulate a response to.

"A cigarette, a piece of candy, a loaf of bread," Antonio says, slapping the back of his hand into his palm for each item, "any of those things are twenty times more evocative for the recipient! A cigarette, *che*, a cigarette is a symbol between men. The invitation matters much more than the act of giving. When you offer charity, you justify poverty. You give and you disappear, and then you go back into your affluent world with a false sense of having helped someone."

"Money is a symbol between men, too. Listen to you, sounding like every Catholic priest I've ever heard in my life with your 'charity justifies poverty.'The charity of those who want nothing in return offends people like you, because you *do* want something in return, just like the church wants pliant souls. Of course you say you have the truth. You want total credulity of your genius, of your higher beneficence."

"And you, you Julián, dare to leave behind some poor wretch with your couple of pesos and their immense loneliness, the ultimate loneliness, the loneliness of having something while having no one. I do the opposite. I hugged the man. I looked him in the eyes. And if you had paid more attention, we both teared up. What you witnessed was a uniquely humane moment."

My adrenaline's up, heartbeat accelerated. If his intention is simply to provoke—and this is the angriest I've been with him since we've met—then he goes too far. I'm willing to endure idiosyncrasy, even egomania, but this pretending to grandiose philosophy when really he's just acting like an asshole is too much. I stare him down. Part of me wants to cast him aside, leave him here under the weight of his own bricks while I go away somewhere else. Staring into his eyes I see confidence, yes, confidence nearing on pompous authority, but I see something else, too. I see lack.

"Come on," I command.

I cross the street and go into a *casa de empanadas*, order a dozen cheese and onion and two large bottles of beer. Not until I turn to leave the shop do I see he's followed me, waiting just outside. I exit with my purchases and motion brusquely with my head for him to follow. We retrace our steps back to the man on the sidewalk, sitting on his cardboard rug with a lit cigarette. Somewhat to my surprise he's not so indifferent this time, nodding his head in a small greeting.

I hold up the bag of food. "Do you mind if we sit with you?"

He still says nothing but scoots back to make room

for us.

I sit and unpack the empanadas. Antonio, with some effort, lays the bricks down and takes a seat. He watches my movements with the same smugness as always, but he's following my lead and that's all I require of him for the moment. I give each of us two empanadas on napkins and we eat. I open the first beer, take a swig, pass it to the man. He looks me in the eye as a modest thank you before taking his drink. He is filthy, smells awful, and drinks from the bottle with a bit of empanada in his mouth. He passes it to Antonio.

"*Gracias, amigo*," Antonio says and drinks without hesitation.

We pass the first bottle around and then move straight into the second. By now we're all feeling good, better with each swig, even having a bit of fun. Antonio has turned into a chatterbox again, and we just sort of look at each other and smile the way kids do when they hang around drinking soda at a street kiosk. The man doesn't talk, but he seems engaged in the conversation, even entertained. The beer runs dry and it's time to go. Antonio stands and says to our friend, "Come on, *carajo*, get up and give me a hug."

He does so. It isn't a pretty hug, not exceedingly natural or trusting, but it does occur. I open my arms and embrace him as well, afterwards giving him a few coins. I turn and see Antonio taking off his shirt and shoes.

The man is suddenly animated, shaking his head and not accepting the clothing proffered to him, insisting Antonio not give it to him. But he puts it on the ground and leaves it with him nonetheless, picking up his ridiculous bricks and saying several flamboyant goodbyes. We walk away, Antonio shoeless and shirtless, waving.

We walk in silence for a bit, drunk and slightly woozy. I still think Antonio's an asshole, but for now I've let it go.

"Another drink?" he says.

"Please."

"These damn bricks are heavy."

"Want some help?"

"Now why do you say that, *che*? You already know I don't work with it if I don't carry it. Stop being so fucking polite and allow people their convictions."

He sits at one of the outdoor tables of a café. I hesitate. He has no shirt or shoes.

"What are you doing? Sit down!"

I do as he says.

The waiter comes by.

"My apologies, sir, but without a shirt I'm not allowed to serve you. I'll have to ask you to leave."

Antonio smashes his fist against the table hard enough to make everything rattle, a couple napkins fluttering to the ground.

"Sir…"

"Here," I say, "I'll give him my sweater."

I take it off and hand it to him. Antonio puts it on inside out, grinning like a mischievous little boy.

"Better now?"

The waiter sighs, shakes his head. "Fine. What do you want?"

"Two beers, please," I rush to say. "Thank you so much."

"Everything is just appearances," Antonio says once he's gone. "Now you see I'm suddenly no better than our friend."

The waiter comes back, slams the bottles down angrily against the table followed by the check.

Antonio laughs. "Suddenly I'm just a dirty savage. No one knows anything about anyone's past at first glance. We're an instant photo. I could've been mugged a minute ago, or you could be a relative of mine taking me out of the looney bin for a walk and a meal. Doesn't matter. The present judges and condemns, always much crueler than the past or the future. What saves us is our past and our hope. That's why I'd rather live in a world of memories and dreams than of successive moments."

I sigh. "Goddamn you, *che*."

He holds out his bottle. "*Salud*."

We'll drink now and suffer later.

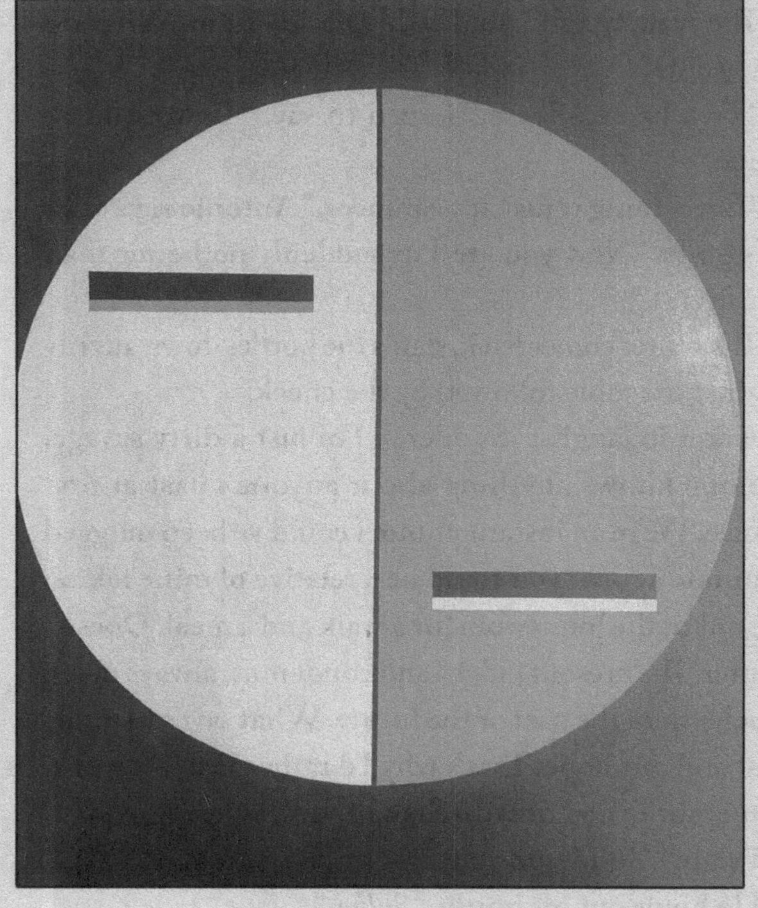

XII

Antonio and Jezebel left together around noon without telling me where they were going or when they'd be back. They simply opened the door, said an abrupt goodbye, and left me to my exclusion. As for Abel, I don't feel his presence in the apartment today.

Except to sleep, I haven't been up in the mezzanine for days. I look up and see the door hanging slightly ajar, a pale light emitting like that of a laboratory. I approach the stairs, lay a hand on the balustrade, grip it hard enough to turn my knuckles white. I go slow, an indistinct echo rumbling within the walls, the black iron sounding under each footstep. The door opens and light spills out. The mezzanine is full of still, silent easels covered by black tarpaulins like cadavers. There are corners full of street debris and broken racks, brushes and paint scattered across the floor. I look behind me. Downstairs, the apartment is dark. There's an easel which stands closest to the door, ahead of the others. The black tarp hangs over the form of a large rectangular canvas. Under the showering fluorescence, I move toward it and remove the cover. There's a sudden pain and I recoil but when I open my eyes the painting is still there, even closer than before. I commit unthinking sacrilege and run my hand across its texture.

A huge eye in the center… stuck with a needle bent into the shape of an S. The marred face stares ahead with empty vision. Blood drops down the cheek in a single dark rope of viscous, caterpillar-like slime that, from within, oozes about into changing forms. The face is pale as marble and gleams even more so in the light, lips bluish, the stabbed eye black, full of blood and pain. The background is a brightly colored pattern of plantain trees, palm leaves, among the vegetation a miscellany of tiny objects, guns, swords, mallets, ropes, chairs, plugs, grenades, kitchens, etc. What does this burst eye want to show the world? An eye is used to search, discover, but to reveal it's an unwieldy tool, mostly incapable of subterfuge or conceit. But there's a tear too, leaking clear and crisp from the eye's edge, fleeing the torrent of shifting blood.

I sit in a chair before the easel, noticing tears on my own face.

My eyelids fall. I hear a voice.

"Take this towel and dry yourself off."

"Who is it?"

"Enough with that now. I just need some answers."

A face with glasses.

"The sum of thirty-two plus nine is?"

"Forty-two."

"Are you sure about that, Julio?"

"Yes."

"Mm. How many days are there in a year?"

"360."

"I'll repeat, are you sure that's your answer?"

"Yes."

"Let's try this. The sum of two plus two is?"

"Five."

"Julio, look at my hand here. What do you see?"

"Two fingers."

"So, if I add two more fingers, like this, you know that two plus two is four, right?"

"Yes…"

"So then two fingers plus two fingers is?

"Five."

"Very well. How many units in a dozen?"

"Twelve."

"That's right, good. So how many plums in a dozen?"

"Eleven."

He moves his head to the side, says a few words into a thin table-mounted microphone. My eyes remain closed and still I see.

He clears his throat. "All right. After August comes…?"

"September."

"Today is?"

"August 2nd."

"In a month it will be…"

"November 2nd."

"But if August is followed by September…?"

"Yes?"

"Then in a month it will be…?"

"November 2nd."

He looks at me, eyes demeaning. I want to stab them. I look around me for something.

"Relax, Julio, there's nothing there."

This man with the glasses seems to have come out of the eye and I can't get rid of him. He looks at me ceaselessly and I can feel him there, oppressive, expectant. He bothers me. I scratch my own face repeatedly.

"Stop, Julio, there's no need for that."

My cheeks grow hot and raw.

"Stop it!"

Just be quiet. Be quiet.

I stand up, look at the painting. I'm in the mezzanine, alone. The man with glasses never existed. The pain in my face is still there. I go to the bathroom, flick on the light.

What did I do to myself? A long needle is pierced through my lower eyelid. Rivulets of thin red blood streak down my face and neck. My shirt is stained with it. My cheeks are scratched raw. What did I…?

I extract the needle carefully, treat the wound with hydrogen peroxide. Wash my face, put on a different shirt, bandage myself up though my eye is already swollen. The apartment is dark and silent, light still leaking from the door above. I need out.

Leaving, I'm blinded by daytime sun. What's happening to me? I stand there adjusting my eyes. Across the street, under a lush tree, is someone I recognize. A woman with a thin face, pronounced cheekbones above pitted cheeks. She's jotting something down in a small notebook. I see her around all the time, but I've never tried to speak to her. I look both ways and cross the street, hoping to introduce myself, but once I'm there she's gone. The tree stands alone. Anyway, I have somewhere to be.

I flag down a taxi and have him take me to Parque Chacabuco. I knock on a green iron gate. A corpulent man in a clean brown sweater answers.

"So you finally decided to show up."

"Sorry?"

"*Boludo!* You were supposed to be here this time last week!"

"Well," I say, collecting myself, doing my best even if

I'm late, "I'm here now."

He frowns but motions me in. "Fine. Come on."

The state of the house is shameful. The paint is peeling. The drains on the floor stand open with no grids. There are a few flowerpots but everything's dead.

At the end of a long hallway, he opens a two-leaf door, revealing a grayish, spartan room with a desk and two chairs, a table with a white telephone, a floor lamp.

"Look," he says, collapsing heavily into his seat, "we're way behind at this point."

"Yes…" I nod.

He lights a cigarette and looks at me, waiting for me to say something more.

"Well?"

"Could I have a glass of water, please?"

He throws his hands out to his sides in frustration, but brings me the water. I gulp it down.

"Hot day out there?"

"Mm… yes… very hot…"

"Well, look, Julio, as I say, I was expecting you last week, so—"

"But I'm here today."

"Yes. Yes, I can see that, thank you. The point is, you're late, so show me your work."

"My work… yes, I can show you. Just let me… could you remind which work you're referring to?"

"Is there something wrong with you?"

"I mean, I don't think so."

"So then cut the crap and tell me what you managed to get done."

I remain silent.

"That is, *if* you got anything done."

I don't really understand why he's so mad. But I think, too, there's something here that maybe I'm not getting. I came here, and it seems like I was supposed to be here, but…

He slams his fist on the table and startles me.

"Goddammit, Julio, what the fuck did you come here for if you've finished nothing and have nothing to say? Are you messing with me?"

"No! No, I'm not like that guy with glasses who drives you crazy with a million pointless questions, all those—"

"Guy with glasses? What are you talking about?"

He stands from his chair, walks to where I'm sitting and shoots his hand out to steady my chin. He looks into my eyes, observes my face.

"So what are you on then? Crack, fentanyl?"

I shrug.

"Just look at you. You're in a sad fucking state. Honestly, I blame myself for hiring you in the first place. I knew there was something up when we met."

"I'm here today!"

"Yeah, you're here today. But you won't be here again. Get up."

He grabs me by my shirt collar and pushes me out of the house with the strength of a bear.

"Get out! And you can take it as a given that you won't be working in this neighborhood anymore!"

"Do I work here?"

"You've gotta be kidding me."

"You… you haven't paid me yet…"

He starts to laugh, flicks his cigarette out into the street, laughs all the way inside as he closes the gate behind him. I look around. People are peering through windows, trying to see what's going on.

These financial people are brutes, every one of them. He promised me work. I showed up even though I'm injured. Maybe it's true I came a week late, but how many people never show up at all? As if I don't need money like everyone to pay the rent and buy groceries.

My shoes are killing me. I take them off and walk along in my socks. They're red. They look good against the gray of my pants. Across the street I see the same woman as before, standing alongside the man with glasses.

"Hey!"

They don't notice, deep in conversation. I step into the street.

"Hey!"

A car horn, a squeal, and an impact like a paper bag crumpling.

Blackness. Pure and deep. I hear, in the distance, noises, rumors, the banging of pots and pans. I'm urged to walk forward. I extend my hands in front of me but see nothing. Finally I glimpse somewhere far ahead of me a room full of light. Once I'm about ten meters away I can see it's a courtroom. Seven figures adorned in white wigs and red robes await me behind the high wooden bench. Someone brings me a chair. There's a halo of light.

"Will the accused plead innocent or guilty?"

"Accused?"

A man comes rushing in. The man with glasses. He takes a seat next to me, pats me on the shoulder.

"Sorry to be late, Julio."

"Let's begin," says the judge seated at center, face grim and skeletal within his oversized red collar, wig condor-like. "Having studied the case against Julio Von Artens, it is the recommendation of the court that the accused—"

"Sir?" I inquire, "what do you mean accused?"

"Julio," the man with glasses says into my ear, "don't interrupt."

"Once more," the judge proclaims, louder, "it is the *decision* of the court to condemn Julio Von Artens to that of Sisyphus."

"A quick inquiry, Your Honor?" the man with glasses interjects. "Will Mr. Von Artens be allowed to keep his red socks?"

All the judges lean toward one another in a flurry of whispered conference. They seem to arrive at an agreement and the judge responds, "We find red socks to be inadmissible. We will, however, make an allowance for the convicted to paint his feet red, if he so chooses."

The man with glasses bows his head, snaps his fingers. Two men dressed like him appear, much smaller, remove my socks and begin to paint my feet and ankles red with two tiny rollers.

"The boulder," continues the judge, "will be of standard weight and dimension…"

Another interruption: "If I may, Your Honor? Round, of course?"

"Do you suggest we are cruel, Counsel? It will be round."

The man with glasses nods, satisfied with his own thoroughness.

The sentence is completed and the gavel falls. My bespectacled counsel pats me on the shoulder. "Well," he says, "all things considered, it could've been worse."

He goes to mingle with the group of magistrates. Two more copies of himself lead me to my cell and shackle me there. I begin to fade away. Darkness again. Everything hellish. My lungs are on fire, legs two inert columns. I try to cry but find myself laughing. What a relief. It all went off without a hitch. Above me, constellations.

Cold, unattainable diamonds. I try to reach them but they're only tears. When will Antonio and Jezebel be back? Jezebel. I miss Jezebel.

My legs ache.

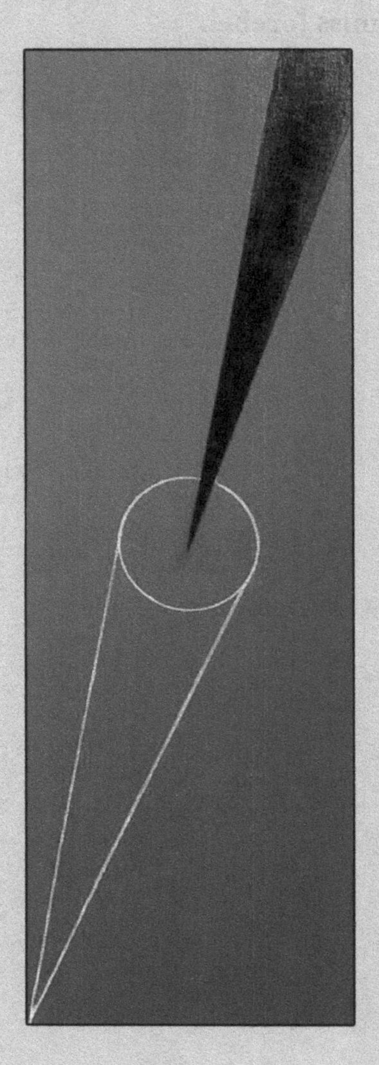

XIII

The apartment is full of people. I don't know whose party this is, but the music is loud and drinks—red and white wine, vodka and absinthe—circulate everywhere. There are kids here who look like they're not even out of university yet, old men and women in outdated clothes. No one told me about this. I don't have the slightest idea what the occasion is, but Jezebel is more intensely beautiful than I've ever seen her before. She has on her blue silk dress and black pearl necklace. Tonight, she's all smiles and charm. Sadness, melancholy, or worry are all for some other night; she's banished all that from herself, reveling in the crowd. Despite her not having noticed me yet, I've done nothing but track her through the party. The mezzanine, too, is full of people. They're laughing up there, clapping and cheering and giving toasts. Up there, in my room!

I'd like to go up, but the sound of Antonio cursing and laughing loudly prevents me. Maybe it's just habit at this point; maybe I can't bear the thought of sparring with him like always, only now in front of an audience. There's a good chance this whole thing is for him.

I wander around a while, not bothering to strike up any conversations but just watching Jezebel from afar. Seeing her interact with so many people is surreal to me, for whatever stupid reason. Once or twice her eyes stray in my direction and I find myself waving, though neither time was she even looking at me. A man of maybe fifty approaches her during a lull in conversation, whispers something in her ear. She nods. The two of them disappear through the door to her room. Her back, the last thing I see. I go to the kitchen, pour myself a scotch. After three shots I'm feeling more relaxed. Everything continues to swirl around me. I'm just standing here, another drink in my hand, watching it all. For nearly an hour no one notices me until a thin, awkward sort of guy walks up.

"You okay?"

"Yeah."

He nods. "Are you a painter, too?"

"Me? No."

"So you work for a charity organization, then?"

"No."

"Are you a, um"—he clears his throat—"are you a

taxi boy†?"

"What?"

"You don't have to tell me if you don't want."

I rub my face, irritated. I notice Jezebel's door open again. She steps out fixing her cleavage. Right behind is the man, fixing his hair.

"Who invited you?" the guy asks me.

"Does it matter?"

"Not at all."

More than just awkward, he's a mess. His shirt is dirty and his breath stinks. And I notice, also, that he's barefoot.

I say, "Things aren't going so well for you, are they?"

Offended, "What exactly gave you that impression?"

"Forget it."

He lights a cigarette, assuming a smug demeanor and blowing smoke almost directly in my face.

"You're definitely a taxi boy."

"I already told you. I'm not."

The first few bars of "Panchito, el Che" by Tito Puente start up and everyone gets excited at once and starts dancing. The guy reaches out and takes my hand, beckoning me to dance with him. I'm not exactly sure why—maybe the fact he's the first person to pay attention to me all night, maybe that I'm burning for Jezebel with no recourse—but I go along.

---

† Term used for male prostitutes.

I continue to hear people in absolute hysterics upstairs. I catch glimpses of Jezebel mingling. Meanwhile, this guy dances like he's having a seizure, all spasm and no rhythm. Long before the end of the first song he's sweating. Genuinely, he's a bit disgusting.

Smiling and nearing in, he says, "You're a taxi boy."

"For fuck's sake, *che*."

"So why are you dancing with me, then?"

Unfortunately, it's a good question. He tries placing a hand against my hip, moving it up toward the side of my stomach. I happen to see Jezebel looking at me for the first time. Her lips arch and her tongue runs between them slowly while her hand goes in and out of her neckline. Everything is completely bizarre.

Nonetheless, as soon as our eyes meet, I abandon the man out on the dance floor. I hear him protesting as I leave. I lean against the same wall as her. For a moment, a crowd gathers around us. I smile at them. They smile back. Of all these people, there isn't one who's well-dressed, and their smell is rank.

"How nice to see you, Julio," she says.

"What is all this?"

She gives me a funny look. "A celebration."

"Of what?"

"Whatever you want. It's a party, you idiot."

"What time did all this start?"

"As soon as you started enjoying it."

The crowd that had gathered around us seems to have dispersed. I can't help myself—"Jezebel, who was that guy?"

"What guy?"

"Don't play dumb."

"I'm not. There're a million guys here."

"Then you…"

A flash of recognition crosses her face. "What are you saying, Julio? Are you judging me?"

"I— no, I couldn't judge anyone."

"Are you sure? Because it sounds like that's exactly what you're doing. And what are you doing watching me, anyway? Is it even possible for you to lie to yourself this much? You're covering your eyes because you don't want to see what's going on."

This house, this world, was something much bigger than I could have possibly imagined at the outset. I'm lost in it.

"Is Antonio gonna be up there partying all night?"

"What do you care?"

"Well, it *is* my room, Jezebel."

"If you want sleep you'll have to go to a hotel. Here, we celebrate. Anyway, I'm pretty sure Antonio already invited Claudita to spend the night."

"And you?" I venture. "Where will you spend the night?"

"I'll sleep anywhere. That's never a problem."

"Would you spend it with me, then?"

She puts her hand on my face and kisses me. Aggressively, but she kisses me. Then, just as suddenly, pulls away.

"You're selfish, Julio."

It's said without anger, only pity.

"What do you mean?"

"*Chau, lindo*[†]. Ernesto's waiting for me."

She turns and goes. I watch as, only a few paces from me, she takes the waiting hand of a frumpy, obese man. As they walk away together, I see him move his hand down onto her blue silken ass and squeeze it.

I'm sick of music.

And yet out of the shadows comes the same idiot from before, now dressed head to toe in leather. Again, he takes my hand and leads me out onto the dance floor with him. I dance without understanding; I'm sure he understands everything but has no intention of explaining. I somehow, amidst all this, can hear snoring—a periodic bass rumbling through the din—along with screaming, cursing, laughing. The guy closes in and says, "How long have you been doing this for?"

I tell him to shut up, but he just keeps dancing. He continues his awful, spasmodic routine, sweat becoming gray, thick, slimy, sliding down his face and onto the floor, onto his leather suit.

[†] Meaning roughly, "handsome."

"Maybe I always was…"

"And how much?" he asks.

I don't listen anymore. I dance, but I want it all to end. It would be nice to be Hölderlin in his tower. I want solitude, but the only substantial solitude is unattainable desire. As for common everyday loneliness, I have plenty right here.

XIV

I decided to follow Jezebel. I know I shouldn't, but I can't bring myself to barge into her life directly. In any case, she won't allow it. Since meeting her, she's kept me at a strict distance. I know nothing of her beyond our conversations in the apartment. In my mind she's a secretive house surrounded by a massive garden maze shrouded in growth, and she invites me only just past the front door. I have to see what happens in her world. I have to, and I don't know how to do so other than furtively. I'll find a point unguarded by her, sneak in when she least expects it. Then I'll see her for what she really is, not just what she shows me when armed with anticipation. For ten minutes now I've followed her through the morning crowd. I hide under signs. I even, in case she looks my direction, bought a newspaper to hide my face, as if this were some old secret agent noir. She does turn around every now and then, like she senses she's being pursued, but it can't be. She presses on, along with my need to follow her. She doesn't give the impression of trying to throw anyone off her trail; but why should she? The morning is heavy, full of humidity and soot, sun hanging above in a blue vault. A trio of flat clouds are strung up immobile. Below, Buenos Aires is frantic. All moves, seemingly without logic, as with two homeless men shifting between benches in Plaza Lavalle. Jezebel strides ahead. She's beatific, blue star in coldest night, rich vein of gold in an exhausted mine. I hold my hands as tense fists in my pocket, sweating even though I feel cold. An empty cold. People look at me, frowning, annoyed by my appearance somehow. I didn't shower this morning and have no idea how I'm dressed, but I don't care. My sole purpose is to follow her. She turns here and there, and at some point I'm no longer sure whether I'm merely trailing or giving chase. I conceal myself behind a destroyed payphone; I talk to a newsstand clerk; I duck into a kiosk. I start to realize everyone notices me, despite seeming like they'd rather not. There are men with glasses everywhere, women whispering in their ears. I don't lose sight of Jezebel, a floating yellow blouse dotted with red flowers. She stops at a huge bifold door and rings the bell. Again she seems to glance in my direction, but I conceal myself behind a car. The door opens and she disappears into the three-story building. I read the sign. It's a non-governmental organization for the homeless. A soup kitchen. I attempt to go in but neither door opens. I stand there, agitated, sweating, rubbing my face and squinting against the heat. A woman passes, says something in an empathetic tone, something about not for another half hour still… I go into the café across the street, take a seat by the window. The waiter drops a cortado in front of me and for some reason demands I pay right away. I toss a few crumpled bills onto the table and he stalks off. I stir the cup a long time. When finally I sip it, I find it's disgusting. I beckon him back.

"Yes, sir?"

"This coffee…"

He has no reaction.

"This coffee…" I repeat, gaze getting lost in the window. A bit of sweat runs rapidly down the bridge of my nose.

"What about it?"

"It's awful. Way too sweet."

"You put the sugar in, sir."

"I put—? But I saw you bring it."

"Are you all right?"

"Yes… why…?"

He stares impatiently.

"Yes… yes… I'm a little tired, but…"

"Anything else?"

"Maybe just a glass of hot water, if you would."

He goes back behind the counter, says something to the cashier and they both break out laughing. A cloud moves in front of the sun and suddenly my reflection resolves in the window. My hair is greasy and tangled all to one side. The corners of my eyes are filled with crust that resembles coarse salt. Snot hangs from my nose in two thick stalactites. I have on my blue blazer but no shirt. I rush to button it but that's not going to help. The waiter brings the water. This time my head is pointed at the table in shame.

"They open in ten minutes…" he says.

"What?"

"They open in ten minutes. You can take a shower, get some breakfast."

I look at him.

"It's nothing to be embarrassed about. I lived there a few months once, back in 2001."

I give a shameful, grateful smile and he leaves me be.

Little by little, people start lining up in front of the NGO door. I watch, sipping the terrible coffee.

It must be that Jezebel does some humanitarian work. Yes, maybe helps with the cooking or something. In the end, she's an idealist. She helps and helps and helps. I breathe raggedly, feeling jealous—of what, of whom, why?—and I can't stop moving my feet. I blow my nose and see snot dripping from my fingers, realizing I didn't even use a napkin.

The minutes go by, and I feel I have no other option except to go stand in the line, forming fast now.

I find myself between a young guy blinking obsessively, scratching his chin till it's raw and an old lady reeking of garlic, legs wrapped in varicose veins.

"First time?" she asks.

"How do you know?"

"You're *looking* everywhere, dear."

"I'm a little nervous."

The young man turns around, laughs, his mouth containing only two teeth.

"That's Alejandro," she says. "He taught tennis in Olivos a long time ago." She contemplates him tenderly.

"He was a tennis pro?"

"Life is strange. I was a math teacher at Vieytes[†]."

I look down at my feet.

"Do you like mathematics?"

I shrug. I'm looking forward to seeing Jezebel…

"It's precise science… important for engineering, physics, all that stuff…" She extracts a red handkerchief from her bust to wipe the sweat from her neck. "Of course, for understanding life, it isn't worth a damn. Life is irrational."

"I'm hungry," interrupts Alejandro, his speech like that of a child's. "Yesterday I slept at the train station

---

[†] Refers to Escuela Hipólito Vieytes. The building is one of the oldest in the neighborhood of San Telmo.

and some kids stole my jacket. I'll trade with you."

"What are we trading?"

"My shirt for your blazer."

I take off my blazer; he gives me the shirt. It fits but it's filthy, black stains and cigarette burns along the collar.

"That was a nice gesture, dear."

"What was it you said about life being irrational?"

"In life, six plus six is thirteen. Nothing's what it seems, and misfortune catches you at any moment."

Her eyes grow unfocused as she launches into a story, though her cheery smile never leaves her, face frozen with singular emotion.

"I was teaching and everything was fine, but then came a student who lost her mother and I consoled her and everything was misunderstood, and they dismissed me for abuse or attempting to abuse. And I explained it to them, but as I said before six plus six is thirteen and that's how it went. I couldn't get hired on at another school and my husband left me for our forty-year-old neighbor—that might sound old to someone your age, but he was sixty, mind—and then I was by myself and the bad became worse and you see how it ended up."

"I'm sorry, señora."

"But don't be so formal, dear. Give me a kiss."

I move to kiss her on the cheek, but she turns and her lips crash into mine. The smell and taste of garlic is sickening, though her smile at the end gratifies me.

"…ah… that was a nice gesture… a nice gesture, dear."

"I'm hungry!" Alejandro complains, louder this time, clutching his belly.

We go on waiting. The lingering garlic taste is unbearable and the shirt, when I look again, is in complete tatters. Everyone's growing impatient and begins clapping in rhythm to get them to open. Shouts rise from the back. There's the sense the line might turn into a mob soon.

Finally, at the point of greatest possible tension, someone turns a key and the doors swing apart. We gush inside, herded down a narrow corridor with white walls and a black tile floor, ending up in an enclosed concrete patio filled with long tables. I don't see Jezebel anywhere though I'm looking around like a lost child. I sit down or they seat me. Someone approaches, takes down my information. I don't know what I tell him. Honestly, I would say anything. I just want to see Jezebel. Garlic smell sticks thick to me, like grease.

Very quickly the place is crowded. Conversations mingle and it's loud. There's laughter, but also the cries of little ones for whom life has become an inescapable thirteen. Someone at the next table over loses consciousness and two men in white uniforms carry away the unwieldy body. His spot at the table is immediately filled by a teenage boy who already has the face of an old man. He grows downwards, towards the grave. He is already a root.

XV

There's a knot right below my diaphragm that's killing me. It hurts a little to breathe. I'm pacing up in the mezzanine, Abel sleeping on the floor and snoring with the regularity of a metronome. Antonio left late last night and I'm only too glad he's yet to return. Jezebel, I'm sure, is downstairs making tea, drinking it in the garden with the voice of Fitzgerald running through her head. And Abel— well, I don't think of him much anymore. He is, as always, totally inert. A snoring dead man. He seems calm, calm enough I don't wish to bother him with my presence. Then again, how can you bother someone who isn't alive?

There's a familiar sickness rising in me. I've been coughing up phlegm again and pacing around like a man in a cage, but I don't want to go out. The idea of a crowded street disgusts me. There are times when I don't think I'm much of a social being at all. I haven't been able to find what I need in other people for a while now. Something's preventing me from making a connection. I'm confused—do we live and then die, or are we dead first and then live only to die again? Eternity is a villain for those who ought to be living on a day-to-day basis. What's the point of everything if I'm just a body rotting? I'd like to see life as Antonio does. Just mock everyone and everything and simply not give a fuck about it all. Like me, he's a storm that never subsides, though he's a hurricane that destroys while I'm just a hovering cloud that wets everything.

I stare out the window and it starts to rain. The sky twists between whitish grays and grayish blacks, mixing and bursting into silver expanses that let down lightning and cracking explosions. The cobblestone of Calle Defensa shines like silicate. The street corners are empty and the glass of the window is cold. My fingers slide down it and leave two ephemeral traces. There's something entrapping in the rainstorm, a tragic melody undergirded by the dead man's snores. The rain taps against roofs and windows, Buenos Aires having turned gray as a lamentation. Why fight loneliness, something that's merely an inseparable component of life and death? Because life is a dream, and dreams exist—isn't that true, Calderón? Perhaps life is the dream, death the awakening from it all.

Out on the road, a bus trundles slowly past, its interior lights the pale yellow of a hepatitis patient. I remember, sometimes, in these moments, my days in the philosophy department. I studied, had many convictions (about which I can no longer remember anything other than that I had them). Things began to dissolve, to crash apart into pieces, like a broken mirror. One tries to find a reason for things, even if one is unable to distinguish between what's real and what's not. I look back into those broken pieces and see myself as Fernando Pessoa, enduring his limitless sadness in Rua Dos Douradores, or as the emperor Julian, grieving for his shattered gods, overthrown by the violence of the cult born in Galilee, or as Cybele, contained in Magna Mater. Belonging is everything, but loneliness is what I know. I seem to belong to this apartment, but it doesn't belong to me.

The loft is unusually cold. The walls, windows, doorknobs… everything the temperature of death. Despite what Antonio says, I would like to live in a succession of moments, with the immediacy of an animal. When the mirror cracked apart, I did my best to put it back together with Occam's glue, which for me took the form of the logic of numbers, of things earned and lost, invested or liquid, or merely theoretical. One can at least keep track. A few figures are lost here or there, not everything always adds up, but what is it all anyway? Tally marks and comparable values. So I did put it back together, I pieced it all back into a whole. I lived with Susana, I worked, and I tried to overlook the cracks, the glue holding it all together. But it could only hold for so long, I suppose. Just as the rain outside might subside momentarily—the trees ceasing to shake, trash to fly out of the bins—in an instant gray turns to black, the skies burst, lightning blinds the eye and the birds seek cover. Once more the city becomes paralyzed, a conglomeration of wet walls and confused currents. The mirror, too, held for a moment before bursting, and alongside Pessoa, Julian, Cybele, I see myself in Antonio, Jezebel, Abel. I sometimes feel, truly, that if I could breathe with their lungs and see with their eyes I might understand what I can't as myself. Maybe they aren't so important, but don't all important things begin with insignificance? If not, how to explain all the time Borges and Van Gogh wasted on trees?

Rain. Outside there's nothing. Nothing saturated with nothing. An immense, indecipherable absolute. Numbers. If an individual person is the final unit of loneliness, how can it be measured against a city where there is no one? Can anyone, then, feel alone? Once, a long time ago, I was in Paris. Loneliness harassed me there, too, not just here in Buenos Aires, its facsimile. Clearly numbers don't work for all things. They do not, for instance, reveal hope as humanity's most pious lie, or time as an honest executioner. They do not calculate for the fact that we deny everything until at last we deny ourselves, nor that we love life because we desire it in all its fullness but hate it because it surpasses us. One dies, and then everything goes on just the same. The *diariero* goes on selling newspapers, office workers find themselves at their desks. The egoist goes on living right alongside the philanthropist. Why undergo all this madness if the reason is simply tedious and stupid? God is not love, it is only cruelty and future promises. If I were Antonio or Jezebel—stoics against the burden of existence—perhaps I would be dignified.

I have a flash of inspiration—something fleeting, the kind of thing you might write or paint so you can hold onto it. The calm of a prairie. Inexhaustible green lost off into every horizon. Sunlight turns to beams as it filters through barges of cloud floating through pure blue sky. A roof of corrugated metal, tiles, and straw that shelters a man as miniscule in the middle of the field as a spider in a bathtub, lost down the drain as soon as the faucet opens. Is that tiny man any less confined than I am here in this loft full of cold canvases? Just a waking dream-ideal, a momentary escape, an original image in which I float with absolute calm because I am subtracted from the process entirely, floating instead in indeterminate space, breath coupled to my heart. As soon as you touch it, paint it, render it in some way, it's destroyed. The only way to live is not to feel, and not to feel is not to live.

The calm of a prairie. Inexhaustible green lost off into every horizon. Sunlight turns to beams as it filters through barges of cloud floating through pure blue sky. No fog, no haze. Beams that bathe everything, the beautiful, the ugly, the alien, the known… A tiny house beside a tiny silo. Who is that person down there? Precisely what I want and what I will never attain.

XVI

"**J**ezebel, didn't I tell you a million times this is a nude?"

"I thought it would be better to paint myself white so you have a clean canvas."

"Clean— ? Are you fucking kidding me?"

He takes a frustrated drag off his cigarette, already burnt close to the filter, and looks at her intently, eyes shrouded by an upward-flowing curtain.

"Don't look at me like that."

He wets a rag and tosses it to her. "Take that paint off."

She doesn't question, just begins to scrub; pale pink appears beneath the white.

Antonio leans up against a wall, his right shoulder shrinking like a *bandoneón*†. I watch them from the top

---

† An accordion-like instrument typical of tango ensembles.

step of the staircase. With my back against the wall, I can see everything through the space between the door and doorjamb. Like a sneaking little kid, I do my best to maintain total silence, stock-still, not breathing too hard so as not to alert them to my presence, observing their relationship.

"Hurry up," he says, wringing the rag out and rewetting it for her.

At first her skin is red and irritated, but little by little it settles and she's left standing naked and fragile as carved crystal. She lies on the floor in the fetal position. He tosses his cigarette and takes up his paints, demeanor transitioning from surly and impatient to a peaceful professionalism. He kneels beside her with great, unathletic effort, daubing a fine-stroke brush with blue and beginning, with gentle, focused intent, to apply strokes of paint to her skin. After these first careful marks he works fast, creating an image across her as if she were a reflective surface of liquid beneath a night sky. Her breathing becomes excited a few times as the brush runs along hidden contours.

Once finished he moves away and her arm extends, as if wanting the hand and brush to return.

"Don't move."

She returns to the position he painted her in. He steps back, evaluating the image. He lights another cigarette with her on the ground before him. Seemingly satisfied, he goes to the easel and begins to make marks, fast and flowing marks, almost reckless, but after only two or three lines I can already see the curves of Jezebel's huddled body coming to life with impressive verisimilitude. He goes on, working with a speed and accuracy that's seemingly impossible. She appears on the canvas almost by incantation. Down on the ground, her body emits a halo—as if she were spotlit, perhaps, but it isn't that, it's something else, something at the edge of perception. After a few minutes the silence in the room grows cathedreal, overwhelming, so much I can hear my heartbeat in my ears. Jezebel has become Ishtar, Antonio a Herodotus of painting. He tells what no one can tell. Images reflected in the mind by capricious sight, though sometimes they seem all too ordinary. Doesn't the eye see water reflecting in the drought of the desert? There's something in this scene—the painter painting the painted, painting the thing that will be looked at—which moves me more than the final product ever could. There is something of the fury of the universe in it, something that conjures in me a soup of archetypes. What cruel demiurge or mad Sophia created space between bodies, space which can never be eradicated or overcome? My love for Jezebel is disquieting, a pure but also frightening love. You can possess your own desire, but never the object of that desire.

The thought of my own indivisibility, and of Jezebel's,

plunges me into a lonely realization. I would like to believe experience can be encompassed and held onto, but even Antonio's abilities, formidable as they are, fall far short. What is a representation other than an act of momentary interpenetration, a frantic and simple intercourse? As in love, it's the most we can aspire to. And afterwards, after the hugging, kissing, orgasm, moaning with caress, comes renewed separation. The dream collapses, the mirage is revealed to be the same dry desert as before, a desire of the mind that kept you moving forward. There's a phenomenon that occurs amongst the profoundly hungry or thirsty—the memory, even just the description, of food or water, can satiate a small part of the need. This strikes me as something deplorable about the fact of existence. Those who subsist on memories are the same as those who subsist on illusions. Just souvenirs of the mind, trinkets kept on a shelf that slowly fade into pieces of meaningless material.

"Dammit, Jezebel, don't move!"

His voice jolts me.

"You have to hold the position! If you move so much as an inch, a centimeter, it all falls apart!"

He returns to the canvas, smoke rising from him.

"Hurry, Antonio," she says, vulnerable reflective fetus on the floor, "I'm restless."

The painting goes on for a long time and still I'm here on the top step. Behind me I can hear someone speaking, the voice of a woman. The sound is muffled, and I can't hear what's being said. Sometimes there's laughter. I try not to care, to stay sitting here, to keep my mind focused on what's unfolding in the loft, but I find myself thinking of Pessoa again. An inconsequential clerk in his bland suit, walking to his office in a calm Portuguese drizzle, all surfaces shining in weak sun, imagination and multiple personalities intact within his head and grief wrapping his heart like barbed wire just as it wraps mine. Life is completely absurd. When I find something, I do so only to lose it; when I search for something, I'm hoping never to lose it again. The only final truth of life is absurdity. A flower collapses from thirst in the desert and someone writes a poem about it, then that same poem is used to whip up hate and anger and thousands die because of a few words put to paper. I get tired of being a human being, sometimes. We seem to be little more than a shadow of what we could or should have been. It would be easier just to believe in some god or another, a book full of dogmas to follow and a code of conduct hypocritical as its promise. Antonio thinks of himself as a god, but look at him in there—if he ever expects to escape his demons, to create something pure, he needs *her*. Why should that be? Because for all his angry philosophy and braggadocio, he expects to save this world and overcome death. Not you, Jezebel. You would simply say, with melancholy smile and shining eyes, *To die at last*. That, to me, is dignity. Maybe even a kind of saving grace. Unlike Pessoa, Antonio would not abandon his art in a trunk, uncaring of whether the world ever takes notice. But you would. You believe the world exists with or without you.

XVII

I'm in the garden alone, in the chair where Jezebel usually sits. The apartment has been empty more often lately. Crossing paths with either roommate is increasingly a rarity. Abel has been here the last few days, but it's hardly a consolation to keep company with a corpse. I lean back, exhale a few lopsided rings of smoke, watch them lose shape and dissipate. Something is very wrong, though I can't understand what. I've tried to ignore it, tried to self-medicate with coffee after coffee, cigarettes, alcohol even… a migraine hits me, fulminating like a faraway explosion, dull at first but soon there's the full force of the sound and shockwave. I drop the cigarette and collapse in the chair, forehead between my legs. The pain is vice-like; I can't move. A few minutes later it ebbs away in phases. On the ground, the cigarette has consumed itself, leaving behind a two-inch strip of ash. The migraines were lengthier before, didn't catch me all at once like this. Now they come at sporadic intervals, the pain concentrated in time and intensity. Like having a sharp rock stuck in my shoe, but in my head. Step the wrong way, think the wrong thing, and I end up doubled over in pain.

I take another long drink of coffee and look at my hands. In them is a small notebook with a green cover and yellow pages. I remember. Abel's snoring had been grating on me, breaking the peace and quiet of the house and interrupting my every thought, so I stormed upstairs with every intention of waking him, but even shouting didn't rouse him. He'd chosen an odd spot for his bedroll. He lay in the space between two huge canvases. My efforts to wake him were short-lived. I spotted, atop his suitcase, the well-worn notebook. Now it's in my hands, and no one is around. I put it on the table, light another cigarette. What would Jezebel say if she saw me with this? I don't have to wonder—she would warn me against reading it, remind me there are consequences for any kind of intimacy.

I puff the cigarette and drink more coffee. Am I not allowed to know anything? Even the person I share my own room with? Do I have to just listen to his snoring for the rest of my life and take it as a given? I lift the cover to the first page. The text is written in a careful blue slant.

I'm always the one I'm not, and I'm never the one I am.

I shut it closed.

Who is this person? Who is Abel? How is it possible I've been living here all this time and know nothing about him? I kill the cigarette in the ashtray and pick the notebook up off the table.

But if I'm to understand anything I should start at the beginning. Which begs the question, which one? Was there a beginning at all? I can assign several, if it's a requirement.

Why not the day I came home from school with a black eye and a bloody nose? I looked at myself in the mirror. This boy, the boy in the mirror, the one with the swollen face and a nose bent like the flap of a blazer, was nothing like the one who had left the house only a few hours before.

Another possible starting point was the night Dad crashed the old three-cylinder car. He crashed it into a traffic light at the intersection of Alberdi and Mariano Acosta, head-on. We all ended up in the hospital, Mom, Dad, and I, stitched up and bandaged but not seriously injured.

Yet another might be the night Mom declared she was leaving to buy groceries but never came back. Days later, after dozens of hours spent on the phone by Dad, all her things remained in the house but now seemingly belonged to no one. Dad was a whirlwind of tears, fury, alcohol, violence... bruises and cuts and screams, crying, always crying, never a nurturing or soothing moment. Always crying. I can't help but cry even now.

I look up to the sky, try to get welling tears to roll back into my head. I'm intruding here, but it's all so familiar. I remember the pain of my own father's belt buckle against my skin, trying to trace the origins of my own broken home…

I seem to always write from a place of grief. To be honest, I live better when I feel it, like an addiction, a drug. An emotion that feels comforting, like home, even if it shouldn't, even if it destroys me. It's like being shut inside an oubliette, surrounded by spikes. You can only stay still and safe for so long, and only with the greatest concentration. Eventually there's no greater relief than to give in, allow yourself to be impaled. I can't help but ask, who am I really? The beginning doesn't even seem so important anymore, no matter how precisely or imprecisely it's triangulated. Every time I leave town it's another beginning. This isn't a new insight. Everyone knows the feeling of being able to reinvent themselves when they leave everything behind, maybe for a vacation, maybe just meeting someone new who doesn't know you and who you'll never see again. But how many people really live by that principle? How many people take it all the way to the end? I travel out of town, make my sales pitch here or there, follow the rules and do what's required, but each time I'm someone different.

But the opening to my feelings is never revealed in the middle. There are beginnings, always beginnings, things that happen at the start which must be explained in clumsy words that never represent what's real, just blurred recollections. That's why all beginnings are subjective. I always break into bitter laughter when I hear someone say with confidence that on such-and-such a day or after such-and-such an event they made the decision to become a doctor, an artist, an entrepreneur, etc. No one knows for sure why things turn out the way they do and not some other way. Beginnings and causes and circumstances aren't what is remembered, only the final deciding factor, like a criminal who tries to justify the crime committed by tracing the events of his past, unable to accept that, from the start, he was doomed. Use whatever word you like, fate or tendency or fortune or karma—I will not commit the crime and then refuse my own criminality.

So it's useless, then. I can only describe the final push, the beginning, or whatever illusory name it deserves. I went on a trip with Dad, I don't remember where. He had to go out of town for some reason and took me along. I remember—very clearly, more clearly than his face—that he carried a book of Neruda's poems under his arm during that trip. This was another world, a long time ago. We went to people's doors and rang the bell and offered to sell them encyclopedias. This really did happen. He sold information, smartly packaged. Who would want it? For what reason? One couldn't know, so you went about at random, and sometimes you could sell it and many more times you were told to get lost. His belt buckle used to positively sing *those words! So eventually I took the advice, and I left him one sunny spring morning. The sun washed over me on a hazy run down an unknown road until someone picked me up and dropped me off in Bahia Blanca, utterly alone. What followed were years of juvenile institutes, escapes and captures, but never a crime for all the punishments received. If I won't shy from my own guilt, neither will I from my innocence.*

I want to sleep but I can't. I have to move, have to stay awake, though I'd like to go throw myself on the floor in the corner of this bar and simply fade to black. There'll be time enough for that. Soon I'll be back in Antonio's studio, sleeping next to the roommate I'll never meet but of whom Jezebel speaks so much. In that regard, I'm stuck here in the present, writing about what was and hoping for what will be. Jezebel has told me what she thinks of hope. She believes in the future even if it makes no sense. I admire that. I do, though, think I have a greater understanding of the future than she does. I don't say this with pride—I understand the need for the future, or at least the belief in it. I know I suffer for my own lack of faith, but some things aren't a choice. We live among occurrences that can't be saved or expected. They have no order, and trend always into chaos. The only order is continuous disorder. I don't mean this to be clever, but I can't deny my own experience. I've done what I could to believe, to have faith, in the future. I see what it protects us from, the incredible trick it performs. Suddenly, out of a hideous tangle, it constitutes the field of time, turning it into various discrete mathematical models. Proof of the greatness of belief in the future is that we obey all models simultaneously and it seems to us no paradox. We put time on our wrists and let it swing around in infinitely limited circles. Dialecticians organize time into lines that go forward and back. Poets and philosophers mold it into a gyre, and so on. I have spun in those circles, moved along those lines, and swirled about in the coil. I see the precious humanity in it, the sincere clerics as well as the Jezebels, beautiful and imperfect as in the Bible, who know it's all a lie but invite you in nonetheless, just to go for the ride, just to share something. I like to take their hands from time to time and make believe I share their belief, and I'm grateful to everyone who has ever extended that kind hand, even those I eventually had to let go of. In the end it's never my choice to return to a world of fractals, outside of belief, but I do because I must. And if I must, why not adapt to its boundlessness, become a constantly multiplying phenomenon, expanding and replicating across and through an unpredictable physics? If I stop, I die.

I would like to keep reading but the final sentence of the paragraph is like a barrier. My hands are trembling. There's a migraine forming at the horizon-line of my mind. No, I can't do it again. I rush to the kitchen, reach into the cupboard for the bottle of gin and a glass. I don't want to be alone. Take a shot, two, three, four more… I miss Jezebel, I miss Antonio. Up in the mezzanine, Abel snores and decomposes. Worms crawl through his skin, flies whorl across his body. The man with the glasses takes notes. If I stop, I die… if I stop, I die… throw the glass aside and drink from the bottle… everything is clouded, nothing anchored…

I wake up on the floor of the kitchen beside my own vomit. It's nighttime. Outside, rain patters in the garden. My first thought is of Abel's notebook. I get up, my head no more or less muddled than before, and bring it inside. By some miracle it's not ruined, only sprinkled with droplets easily dried off with a rag. The wind picks up and heavy rain starts to fall, bad enough I have to close the door to the garden. Above the din… snoring. I sigh and shut my eyes tight. Still no one here. After cleaning the floor, I take a seat and open the diary again.

I boarded a bus in Once with a briefcase and left Buenos Aires into a clear horizon. Soon we were in the open country. The sky in the east was a coat of silver crossed by an occasional streak of bright pink or yellow. There were no clouds. Everything was an inseparable unity. The bus was half empty, a passenger in the seat in front of me but not behind. The driver smoked and drove the huge wheel with one hand, the tinny radio playing songs about lost loves and blurry memories. The land unraveled as we sped ahead, flat, unchanging, and tedious for those moving at our speed.

Back in the city, millions of people all awoke at the same time, showered, dressed, went to work. Produced. Went to bars, ate lunch, drank Fernet and beer and coffee and went back to work. They chatted about their sorrows and joys with coworkers and strangers. Then they returned home after another day. That was my life, too. One of those strangers in a bar on one of my lunch hours once left an impression on me by cynically quipping, "If you want to locate the beginnings of human stupidity, it's simple. Just find the person who invented the word 'forever.'"

Daybreak spiders across the open land into a pink dawn, huge, unlimited. I awoke as Abel. I put on a worn suit with green elbow pads. I put on freshly polished shoes with rubber heels. I put on a pair of black-framed glasses. But then what? I boarded the bus. I sat as the red, white, and silver shell ate mile after mile of flat empty road, lost somewhere in the Pampas. I watched birds and cows from the windows. Night stepped aside and dawn introduced the day, and the giant wheel turned and turned. Nothing makes sense; it's absurd. Why did I do it? These humans cannot stop, they must build with unbridled mania and myopia—who will this legacy be left to once we destroy ourselves? Can we be so vain? The universe works at a different pace than we do. Anything explained is temporary and irrelevant in the scheme of things.

I do it to move continuously. I have no other choice. To live obsessively, if such a thing can be done. Be compulsive in all I do. Let everything imbue me without offering any resistance. That and nothing else. Live like a paintre maudit in Modigliani's time. What more can a person aspire to? To live as a flower facing the desert and refusing to dry up and die. I want that stubbornness. Just to move. Move until the end, when the fatigue finally becomes brutal and all minds collapse.

The front door opens. The sound of high heels against the floor. I quickly shut the notebook and hide it away in a little-used drawer. Jezebel, black hair rippling over a dark beige dress, steps into the kitchen.

"Julio?"

"What time is it?"

"Five-thirty."

She sits, seeming tired and indifferent. She is, as always, since the first moment, beautiful, but not untouched by age and trauma. Her visage is that of an orphanage girl made disillusioned well before her time, daubed with a young person's functional dementia of not knowing how or why or when things got this way. She lights a cigarette like a factory laborer after a double shift.

"Your mascara's running…" I say quietly.

She nods, shrugs her shoulders, gives a mirthless, half-apologetic smile. "Are you the only one home?"

"No. Abel's upstairs."

"What about Antonio?"

"I don't know. I haven't seen him all day."

"Then you're the only one home."

I say nothing. Silence lingers between us and grows, extends throughout the entire apartment. The snoring, constant since last night, has disappeared.

She requests (though does not intone it as a question), cigarette balanced between wine-colored nails, "Can you make me an absinthe, Julio."

I do as she asks, retrieving the bottle and paraphernalia. I'm happy to busy myself for a moment. The apartment is so quiet, every sound seems magnified. Cupboards closing, ice cubes softly cracking as they're dropped into water, the clatter of the thin metal spoon. I uncork the bottle and pour the thick green liquor into a clear glass, *glick-glick-glick*; balance the teaspoon across the rim and place the sugar cube on top, sparkling like a fresh snowflake; her eyes follow every movement; finally applying a constant stream of ice water atop the cube. We watch it give way little by little, becoming an uneven rubble of sweet atoms until it's fully dissolved. I take away the spoon and slide the glass to her. She sips it modestly.

"You prepare absinthe so well…"

"A friend from Poland taught me."

The drink relaxes her, replaces her sullen and cryptic bearing with a more amiable one. I watch her undergo the subtle transformation. Her eyes remain glazed, containing tears perpetually ready to fall and make dark streaks across her cheeks. Studying her, I imagine myself a painter, destitute but bearing a pure soul, living without expectations while at the same time enduring a hunger for everything, all things.

"Where were you, Jezebel?"

Some of her renewed attitude drains from her. I seem not to be able to help myself.

"On the street," she says.

"But where exactly?"

She doesn't answer, just sighs and stares at the floor, spinning the glass of absinthe with her fingers.

"Jezebel…?"

"Stop, Julio! Why do you want to hear me say it? Why? Are you ashamed of me?"

I sputter. "No, never—"

"Then why? You know, you should be careful about wanting to know people too much. Because once you get too close, the person you know dies. They're not them anymore, and they never will be again. They're just an illusion of logic, X and then Y and so Z. Is that what you want, Julio? To untangle me in your mind?"

"No—"

"Well, fine. Fine—since you insist on refusing my refusals, fine. You'll get what you want."

"Jezebel, I'm sorry, please—"

"Shh. Julio. Just listen. I'm going to tell you why I do

what I do."

She throws back the entire glass of absinthe without so much as a flinch, looks me in the eyes.

"I had a brother. I had two, but Gabriel disowned me a long time ago, ever since he found out about my 'other' job. My brother's name was Oscar, Oscarcito. He was beautiful, Julio. He had a perfect soul. A soul that made me tolerate men, that made me see what was hidden and alive and feeling in the world. He made me understand kindness. Not niceness, not politeness. Real sensitivity and reverence to what's alive and separate from you, what's fragile and so easily damaged. He didn't kill bugs. He didn't pick flowers from the ground or leaves off trees. He loved everything. He ate no meat back when being vegetarian was an act almost on par with burning the Argentinean flag to most people. He was sickly from the very beginning, a common thing for sensitive souls. He had very bad intestinal problems, which made him pitiably thin, and asthma, too. He fell from a tree when he was five and broke his tibia and fibula bones, and as a result one of his legs became shorter than the other. He found it hard to be around people. Most of his life he didn't interact with the world. Starting at sixteen he turned into a bibliophile and spent so much time alone reading it concerned all of us. He loved art, too. He loved Soutine's paintings and admired Gauthier. He never had a girlfriend in his life, someone who wanted to be with him. I remember when he was nineteen, he was obsessed with a college girl who wouldn't give him the time of day because of his limp, and when she rejected him, he came home just sobbing and sobbing. I thought at the time he was crying over puppy love, but it turned out to be grief for what he would never experience."

She stops, eyes burning holes in me, but it's not me she's looking at. She's trying to hold back tears, but two drops, gray from the mascara, tumble from her eyes, one clinging to her cheek, the other falling silently to the floor.

"After that his life changed. In his mid-twenties he moved to a boarding house and started to paint. He painted nuns and prostitutes. He saw them in a similar light. And of course it said something about the displacement of his sexual affections. He said these two groups of women know true solitude, both sustained by faith. He was compulsive, my brother. Like with his reading, once he became fascinated with something he took it to the limit. He'd sometimes do three paintings a day, eat and sleep very little if at all. There was an incident where he fainted in the middle of a painting, and the prostitute put a pillow under his head and a blanket over him and stole everything of any value she could find. When Oscar invited her back to finish the portrait, he increased her pay. So, as you can imagine, his room inevitably became a welcome refuge for any unfortunate person. His sexual experiences were with those he painted. Mostly the prostitutes, but not only them. He said he'd made love to at least one of the nuns. From the outside, a lot of this is difficult for people to understand. There was a clear element of Oscar's painting that was abusive of his sexual impulses, I won't deny that. But he wasn't violent, wasn't coercive. The people who went to his apartment, either to be painted or just to be around him, did so because being there was different from being anywhere else. I met a lot of people there, many with tragic stories, but we didn't always talk about that stuff. More than anything, what I remember from all the hours I spent with them was a lot of laughing and languishing. And drinking. Oscar had been a drinker since his teenage years, but when he moved to the boarding house he turned into an alcoholic. And for the most part, whoever came was welcome. Though he attracted seedy people, damaged people, junkies and thieves and whores and the eccentric, he didn't attract those who were violent. No one went there because it was some spider's lair or den of iniquity. People went there for a simple reason, which was that they were not judged. At Oscar's apartment, people were completely open about sex and sexuality. They didn't hide it, didn't hide who they'd slept with or their preferences or if they felt horny or not. In the same way, they didn't need to hide their identities. If they were whores they were whores. Nuns were nuns, thieves were thieves. It was a strange environment, but for all that it was absolutely honest. One of the very few completely honest places I've ever experienced. Contrast that to my brother Gabriel's home—an upstanding tax lawyer with solid Catholic morals, a beautiful wife, two healthy children—I never once felt comfortable there. I found their lives riven with insinuations, distrust, unequal expectations and small fears. Maybe you can understand, maybe you can't. I just know how I felt about it. Eventually, Oscar moved away from painting nuns and prostitutes and he took on a different array of subjects. I posed for a portrait, once. In my opinion, one of the best he ever did was a nude of a poor woman from Rawson who'd lost both arms up to the elbow and her right leg up to the hip at the age of twelve when she fell under an oncoming train at Estación Retiro. He painted her in a beautiful sepia color and they, too, had sex. She was a regular presence for a while at Oscar's apartment. He painted men, though I was usually less interested in those. A whole range of broken and unfortunate men. Oscar's fate came as no surprise, as much as I hate to say it. He contracted a brutal case of gonorrhea and ended up in the hospital. During treatment he was diagnosed HIV positive. What followed were endless bouts of excruciating intestinal inflammation and bronchitis, and in short order he died of pneumonia in the winter of 2005. He was young, but he didn't curse his fate. I think, in a certain way, it was scarier to watch him die in so much pain, and with such acceptance, than it was to be him. Anyway, I'm aware how this sounds, but I took a lot of inspiration from his life. That's why I do what I do."

"And…" I ask, "…and… aren't you afraid of what might happen to *you?*"

"A little, to be honest. But I do it anyway. Because I chose how I wanted to live."

Right now, my universe is centered on her. She's opened this strange, ungraspable world to me, this personal history, and I know I wasn't deceiving myself—I love her. I love her completely. But I also know I'm not the only one. I'm just one of many.

"So here's what you wanted, Julio," she says. "I'm a whore."

I simply look at her. I feel purified by her story, reborn in my complete admiration.

I can't think of anything to say so I stand up out of my chair and so does she. I open my arms and she falls into my embrace. She's no longer a garden maze, no longer a house. She's shed her metaphors and mystique and is a real person, a beautiful person, burying her head into my shirt and letting out a fresh round of tears. I can feel myself trembling with something that's not quite nervousness, not quite adrenaline… my hand touches her face and I purge adjectives from my thoughts. I bring her face toward mine. We kiss. Her breath is a dizzy tonic of tobacco and absinthe.

"Julio…"

But words have finally drowned in feeling. Without them there is no longer any resistance.

What dances in the background of it all, though, is another truth, the truth of our love's impossibility, that this encounter with the impossible will soon become a sweet fleeting wound around which we will be condemned to circle forever. I know she fears that punishment—the consequences for having put life and death aside, buckling under the pressure of desire.

Both of us are lying face up on the floor, exhausted. Next to me, her body is covered with a shiny patina, skin still bristling and sensitive, her breasts rising with slight spasms. I see her now in her basic essence, a saintly prostitute; she absorbs sadness, madness, lust and loneliness and anger, violence, shame and fear and guilt, and she recycles it into being, plain and invaluable. A salve rising from society's unconscious. I find myself embarrassed not to have wondered at the other side of her, the promiscuous saint. Maybe I'll know it, someday. Maybe, in another life where all things are possible… for now, our time together is already slipping away. This moment, the moment in the wake of unbridled freedom, already no more than a memory and a sense of immense emptiness, of already missing the most precious thing I had in my life. Her eyes are idle, igneous black. The simplicity of living beauty can't be recreated, not even by the talents of a Raphael or Michelangelo. Even their masterpieces are merely monuments to loss, the loss of an extraordinary moment, and when the monument finally stands before you, even if it towers twelve feet tall, it is nothing but what is already gone. Memory does not work for the extraordinary—it's unrepeatable.

I reach for my pants and extract my pack of cigarettes. I light one and hand it to her. There are tears in her eyes.

"Jezebel… what's wrong?"

She takes the cigarette and smiles. A sad, satisfied smile. Takes a drag and looks away.

I light my own and we blow smoke towards the cracked, water-damaged ceiling.

"I didn't mean to…"

"What does it matter what you meant to do?" she asks.

"I guess it matters to me."

"You're sweet, but I don't need explanations. You should know by now I actually prefer to go without them. What would it change?"

We go on smoking. For some reason I want to say the right words. My mind is racing with words. I don't understand why.

"I've never felt like this before," I say. I don't even know what I mean, but it's true.

Mystic that she is, she knows exactly. "There's no need to tame every impulse. Even if what results is sad, give me what you feel. Be brave and show me who you are. Hiding behind modesty isn't for you, Julio. To make it all into some coherent chain of logic will just kill your thirst for living."

She rests her head on my chest. I feel myself disappearing again. She climbs on top of me, gasps, her lips reach mine and then stay near. She collapses again.

We stay like that a long time, so long her weight is making me suffer against the hard floor, but I don't dare move. I want her here, on top of me, because I know what happens next.

She lifts herself up. "Life is movement, *querido*," she whispers.

"Maybe death is more benign, then."

"Yeah. Maybe." With a mischievous grin she steals another cigarette from my pack as she gathers her clothes.

I stay where I am, on the floor. "Well, if it's all movement, it's too fast."

She puts her toe in my belly button and I flinch. Standing over me, she smiles, clothes in arms, cigarette aflame.

"You'll only find me when you're not trying, Julio.

When time loses all meaning."

"Jezebel…?"

Too late. She's already gone to the bathroom. I'm here on the cold floor alone.

XVIII

Antonio is gone. I haven't seen him for weeks. The mezzanine is full of covered canvases, but the smell of oils and acrylics has vanished. All the paint is dry, cracking, the brushes mangled and unused. I wished he would leave so many times, but now that he's gone it no longer feels like a studio up here. Now it has all the eeriness of an abandoned shed, the desolation of a deserted grandstand. Part of me thought to take up a brush and paint, but it's useless. I admire art, I live and breathe it, but I can't create it. I miss the madness up here. I miss the tyrant who demanded I know all the answers. There never were any right answers, now that I think of it. He just wanted me to obey. Obey the questions.

I go downstairs and make myself a coffee, sit at the patio table. Above, a convoy of massive clouds moves briskly across the rectangular window of sky. My art is my loneliness, rattling around this empty apartment like a crumpled poem at the bottom of a trash can. Even the ghosts have abandoned me. They no longer haunt the corners or the in-between spaces.

Jezebel, too, has gone. The last time I saw her was like a dream just before waking—she emerged from her room wearing a duckling yellow dress cinched at the waist by a wide brown belt, eyes rested and lively, hair washed and flowing. She didn't glance at me, even though I know she saw me sitting there, even though my entire being called to her. She grabbed her keys from the table by the door and disappeared. I had meant to say something, to call her name, anything, but I could do nothing, I could only sit, paralyzed, watching her leave.

So now where am I? Lost somewhere in this infinite, indifferent labyrinth of rooms and chambers. With them gone, it's like the city doesn't know me anymore. I look at the back of my hand. A cluster of veins runs through it like the trail of a plough in soil. Everything stagnates and life is wasted. Shut away in a prison, what good is anything? How can I even know I exist? I haven't been outside in a long time. A human being filed away, silent and unreachable. One begins to abstract, separate from oneself, one's body, even one's mind, becoming a separate entity observing oneself walking endless and aimless about the cell, a detached observer, until even the observer becomes bored and uncertain of their own existence, splitting into an observer of the observer of the subject, a separate and bodiless persona created to validate the first two. And when will the splitting finally end? Or does it ever? Does it just multiply and cycle through an infinite interior?

I've had the sinking feeling for a while now that I misused the lessons of both philosophy and mathematics. Rather than extract teachings, I used them to paper over imperfections and tears in my own personal reality, like a sailor frantically plugging up a leaking hull. An endless cartoon, to be sure—once one hole is plugged, another appears, and the whole thing goes on like that without the sailor ever thinking to just let the ship sink. I see concepts, but not applications. Does that make me insane?

Not so long ago, Jezebel and I were in wild love like something out of a Zola novel. We approached one another, but as soon as we met, we were already moving apart. How can everything be disintegrating so fast? Is it possible to keep plugging the leaks? Artaud, my friend—why not be a body without organs? No need to wait for God. Rid myself of them and untether the ship from the ocean itself, let it float rather than sink. The ship becomes an egg. Memory hatches from it and once more walks about as flesh and blood...

XIX

Now I remember. I remember I finally met Abel. When was this? Impossible to say. Antonio and I were in the kitchen, drinking a cortado. I don't remember when he arrived back home after having been gone so long, or how we ended up in the kitchen together. I remember it was daytime—out in the garden, sun shone down on the pergola and birdsong fizzled in the air. There was the sound of the heavy front door opening, and both of us listened. We could tell it wasn't Jezebel right away. No clacking of high heels or the feeling of her breezy presence. Instead, the air in the apartment became strained, and there was a bad smell. Footsteps sounded, but not those of a normal person. They were measured, mechanical. Step. Step. Step. We looked toward the kitchen door, only partway open. We waited. A figure filled the space, a figure I had only ever seen dead on the floor, now standing at its full height. He looked and saw us but remained in the hallway, standing with uncanny stillness. A voice spoke, flat and indistinct.

"*Buen día.*"

Antonio—grave and unspeaking—looked at him and nodded before turning his attention back to his coffee. I could think of nothing. He was partially obscured; I couldn't make out his features with any precision. He stood there looking through the space in the door for a long time, not moving. He didn't blink. His face wasn't animated by spirit or emotion. Just inertia and an icy stare. Antonio patted my forearm gently.

"He's not really there, *che*."

"Huh?"

He motioned to the unmoving figure beyond the door with his head. "He's already half-dead."

I looked at Abel. He didn't breathe, didn't move his fingers, didn't smile or frown or move his eyes. I could see enough to discern he had large ears, and his face was heavily lined like that of a much older person. Greasy, thinning hair fell across the collar of a rumpled shirt.

"*Con permiso*†," the voice said, slowly turning and climbing toward the mezzanine.

Antonio sipped his coffee, watched the thing go up out of sight. The same unnerving footsteps continued

---

† Meaning, "Excuse me."

upstairs.

"That was the wake. Once he gets up there, he'll collapse and that's it."

"Antonio… what did I just see?"

"What's not to understand, *pibe*? He travels for work. He told me he hates his job and loves the road."

"I read his journal…"

"Mm."

"I had to."

"Well, it's not like you don't have the right."

We went silent again as the sound of footsteps in the mezzanine persisted. Slow, zombie-like.

"Maybe I was wrong," Antonio said. "Maybe this time he's half-alive."

I was looking at the stairs and my mouth must've been hanging open because all at once Antonio stuck a piece of dulce de leche in my mouth.

He chuckled to himself. "In all seriousness, Julián, the end is the beginning. It's as soon as you die that you begin to live."

I shot him a *ha-ha* glare, chewing the pastry. "Just a riddle," I said.

"No riddle. Where do you think life begins exactly? Deep down, everything's a circle. Everything contains everything. Opposites are just the obverse of the same body. Without them there's no shape, no balance or finish. Death is the condition for life to spring anew. So that's why he does it. That's my interpretation, at least. He dies and is reborn, and now life has a whole new set of qualities, a fresh fascination. Each day a new lover, like Don Juan. Can't you understand that?"

"But what if there's another reason?"

"What other reason?"

"Well, we all seek permanence—"

"The grandest illusion of all, *viejo*," he rushed to interrupt, misunderstanding me. "Everything is constant movement. Today you're something, tomorrow you'll be something else. Water flows, condenses, falls as rain, becomes stream, river, and sea, brings life back to broken earth, quenches the thirst of all creatures. Odorless, colorless, tasteless. Flexible, tenacious, patient, thriving, regenerative. Water, *carajo*, understand water and you understand everything! Let life flow through you. Make yourself into a dam and you do nothing but block it."

"Let it all flow through you? So what of art, then? Isn't that a dam? Doesn't that seek to halt something, bring it to a standstill, even?"

"Just a virtual affirmation of one's existence, that's all. Life doesn't care. But look at you, Julián. You want one last shot at answers, that's plain as day, but what more can I tell you? Have you considered that I don't know? The point is, life comes to each of us and says, 'Here, I've bestowed you with the greatest gift. Now do whatever you want with it. The only requirement is that when you die, you recycle yourself into something.' The freedom between the first moment and the last is what matters. I try to do something to justify that gift, which is art. I'm that person who doesn't like to see the gift of life abused or taken for granted. I'm never satisfied with anything, and I always think more can be done. At the same time, I'm well-aware I can't live up to my own standards. That's just me, and you should know that better than anybody."

I sat there, willing to listen forever if only he wouldn't leave.

"But look, *viejo*, I gotta get going. Thanks for the coffee. It was worth stopping by just to see the look on your face when The Corpse walked through the door."

Then he was gone. I was happy he misunderstood me. Antonio always fights what has no answer. Once he'd left, though, my original thought reformed. I remember what Abel said in his journal. *We live among occurrences that can't be saved or expected. They have no order, and trend always into chaos. The only order is continuous disorder. I don't mean this to be clever, but I can't deny my own experience. I've done what I could to believe, to have faith, in the future. I see what it protects us from, the incredible trick it performs. Suddenly, out of a hideous tangle, it constitutes the field of time, turning it into various discrete mathematical models.*

Antonio, even if he professes to the contrary, has faith in the future. He justifies the gift of life because he believes in existence, some ordered consciousness or moral echo. Abel has no choice but to fall back into a world of fractals, a world without beginnings, ends, or anything in between. Which is real? Or do they exist parallel, everything containing everything?

My muscles tense and I freeze in the chair—I can hear Abel's footsteps. That shuffling empty shell is still in the apartment with me…

The small rapturous voices of the birds outside have vanished, replaced by the buzzing of flies. It's cold, and the stink of death overpowers everything. The footsteps move to the spiral staircase. I pound the table with my fist, let out a small laugh that immediately turns to tears. No stopping it. It's just a virtual affirmation of my existence, and what does life care? The sun outside wanes to darkness. The steps clank, one by one. I turn my eye toward the door. I can see the figure reaching the bottom. Abel. Flies swarm over his body. He approaches the door, staring in at me, face covered in shadow. I grip the coffee cup in fear.

"Buen día."

XX

The apartment is empty, silent, dark. Jezebel's copy of *This Side of Paradise* sits out on the patio table covered in cigarette ash and fallen leaves. All the statues and furniture seem different, and Antonio's murals have been painted over. I hear, from time to time, a haunted little feline mewling coming from somewhere faraway, much farther than should be possible. I call the cat's name, but my voice is too weak to fill the space. Wherever it is, it doesn't respond. Upstairs, the mezzanine is a yawning, teetering void. Without Antonio, it's just remains. In a gyre of heavy time thick with broken bricks and plaster dust, he and Claudita and a billion tiny men swirled away forever, leaving behind a final acropolis. Why? What was the point? I wander through the hallways, past silent bookshelves and crumpled silk dresses, tightly shut doors, windows that look out onto nothing but grayness. The plants have been neglected. They lay dead and brown in their pots. I hear something; a voice, but faint. Not the cat, something else. A human voice. I stop, grasping onto the wall as if it will help me listen better. Yes… yes, there are voices… but nothing distinct. A distant din I can't make out, but I recognize the voices of my roommates. Where are they? What room? I call out their names but it's clear my voice doesn't reach that far. Can they hear me, too? It's like I'm not in the apartment at all. Why don't I recognize anything? Not even my own clothes—a blue shirt and pants. What's going on? Why can't I find the door? It's all just a trick—take these books off the shelves, the rugs off the floor, there has to be something behind or underneath. These fucking doorknobs don't move. The windows won't break. What am I, a prisoner? Who's doing this to me? Let me see inside these cupboards, you bastards, where are you all hiding? Is it funny to you? Is it funny to see me scared out of my mind? Lonely and confused? Does it make you laugh? Go to hell, all of you! Every last one! I'm not just some victim! You shouldn't treat me this way; you shouldn't treat *anyone* this way! I'll fucking kill you! I'll tear you apart for doing this to me! You think it's funny, but I'm scared! What if I did something awful? What if I killed someone? What if I killed myself? Would you still be laughing then? Would you even care? Would you? Answer me, you goddamn fucking idiots! *Answer* me!

…the hell with it. I sit at the table. There's an empty coffee cup here, and a book by Guy de Maupesant lying open. I feel dizzy from my outburst, eyes dry and scratchy. Well… it's my own fault anyway. I was the one who peered into the abyss, trying to look around every corner and past every surface. I made the decision, no one else. So who do I have to thank if the abyss peers back? Jezebel warned me. What did she say? Don't get too close. The person I knew is dead. Don't adjectivize everything when you should just be. You can only know the truth once it's too late. How is it she finds such rationality in madness? Sees so clearly through the muck of spirit? She tried explaining it to me. She saw me stumbling in darkness and said, You can't see because you still think somewhere there is light. I remember what a bunch of enlightened professors made of the teachings of Epicurus. Because he dared to state that pleasure leads to happiness, they took him for the inventor of hedonism, even though he also said, very clearly: there is no greater pleasure than the pursuit of goodness. They took the wrong lesson and invented the philosophy they secretly wished he had preached. Like me, they could only believe the part that—perhaps— should make sense, not accepting what isn't quantifiable or empiric. So much in life is paradox and can only be proven by its very confusion. The more we look for absolute explanations, the more we sink into fantasy. I wanted to leave my old life behind, my life with Susana, because I wanted explanations for so much utilitarian morality. That life was a whole universe of explanations, a whole cosmogony of illumination. Maybe I didn't understand the value of answerless questions, the endless reformulation of unknowableness.

So then let it be; it couldn't be otherwise. These three souls had to live over-top one another here in this place, and I was merely a foil to their knowledge. A witness to their existence. All this while Abel slept calmly and Antonio painted his dreams, populating them with symbols and objects and desires so as not to leave the poor creature in utter chaos. Jezebel lived those dreams, walked their worlds with bruised and bleeding skin, changing the pain and ineradicable suffering into whatever was once again usable.

The apartment expands around me. Everyone is gone, but I can still hear their voices.

Muffled and faraway. But if I let go… if I let go, maybe I can understand them…

There's a knock at the door.

I raise my head.

Another knock, less patient.

"Open the door!"

I stand, go slowly into the foyer. Two distorted figures stand behind the beveled glass of the door.

Voice shaking: "Who-who is it?"

"Open the door, Martínez!"

"Mar-Martínez?"

The heavy door swings open and there's no explanation.

XXI

It's been days—years—of interrogations. Endless questions to which I find no purpose. There are three of them, all in white uniforms like ghosts. The man with glasses, always with his green notebook. A woman with a thin face, pronounced cheekbones above pitted cheeks. The third is a bald man, his eyes sunken and sleepless, sagging with dark bags. I sit before them in my blue shirt and pants every morning and listen, responding to their inquiries with single syllable answers. On occasion I find myself wanting to explain something. These explanations seem to discourage them, and their expressions turn grim. At some point they brought in a couple of Antonio's paintings. They lay them carefully atop the table, drill me with a million nonsensical things. "Can you tell us a little bit about these, if you would? About the figures in them? There's this intersexual one here, can you tell us what your inspiration was? Do you view yourself as intersex? How about the tiny men? We like these paintings, we'd like to know more about them. What, in your mind, do these figures represent? They seem to be self-portraits, would we be correct in saying that?"

I sit there, arms folded. "I don't know. Why don't you ask Antonio?"

"So these are Antonio's paintings, then?" the man with glasses asks. "What's your opinion of Antonio's work?"

"He does whatever he feels like. He might as well be homicidal. He's above ego."

The woman poses a question. "And what about you? Do you paint?"

"Me? No."

"But Antonio paints," the bald man confirms. He's insufferable, always leading with his tone of voice, as if he knows the answer he wants from me but won't say what it is.

"That's what I just said."

"You don't find that the smaller figures resemble you a great deal? Why would Antonio paint someone who looks so much like you over and over like this?"

I say nothing.

The woman clears her throat, changes the subject. "Sorry to press you on this, but I'd like to bring up something we've discussed before. The journal you kept. I'd like to know more about Abel, if you feel like you can share."

I swat the question away with a hand in the air, annoyed at their stupidity. "Abel's dead…"

"Abel's dead?" the man with glasses asks.

"Yes!" I shout at them, rising out of my chair. "Yes!"

"Cristian, please…" begs a freckled, brunette woman sitting behind them, someone I didn't notice in the room until now. "Please, just answer their questions…"

I look at her again. "Graciela?"

It's my sister.

"What are you doing here?"

When I say her name, her eyes well with tears and she stands, walks towards me. I back against the wall.

"Ma'am," the bald man says, "please sit down!"

Graciela touches my face, her hands old and worn. Tears run down her cheeks. "Cristian, I'm here."

"Who's Cristian?"

She pulls back.

"Ma'am!"

"Don't you recognize me? You have to answer their questions, Cristian, you have to stop refusing your medication."

"Doctor! Get her away from him now!"

"Please, Cristian!"

"Graciela, where's Jezebel?"

"What do you mean where is she?"

The man with glasses is suddenly behind her, trying to pull her away, but I hold onto her.

"Where's Jezebel?"

"Cristian, stop! Stop!"

"Get someone in here now!"

"What the fuck did I do to Jezebel?"

I push the man with glasses and he crashes into the table, onto the floor. I hug Graciela tight but I lose my balance and we fall down. She's screaming. I cover her mouth to stop the noise. She tears at my hands.

I weep. "What did I do to Jezebel? What did I do? What did I do?"

The door swings open and two men pull me off her like I'm made of paper. My arms are pinned painfully behind me as they drag me from the room.

Who is that woman back there, crying inconsolably? Why does she have so many bruises? And the blood that was on the wall, on her face? How did that happen?

They toss me into a small room. There are paintings stacked against the wall. I smell the familiar jasmine essence of Jezebel mingling with the stink of The Corpse.

"*Mierda*, Julián. Shut up. Stop making so much noise."

On the ceiling are Antonio and Claudita.

"*Callate, carajo*."

I burst into laughter.

A faint voice beyond the door: *Two weeks. Not a day more.*

My laughter dies away. What was all that?

My eyes close…

…I turn onto Avenida Paseo Colón, Avenida Independencia, past Calle Bolívar to Calle Perú. I run across a refurbished warehouse, turned into lofts. There's a handwritten sign outside: ROOM FOR RENT. *I ring the bell and wait, finding I'm a bit nervous.*

The heavy iron gate creaks open, accompanied by a pant of exertion.

"Sorry. This door is so heavy." A slender woman with curly black hair stands before me, eyes, too, black as ebony. She's beautiful.

"Can I help you?" she asks.

"I saw you have a room available?"

"It's 18,000 pesos a month. First two months in advance…"

MORE FROM ZQ-287

PSYCHOLOGY OF TECHNOLOGY TRILOGY
STEVEN T. BRAMBLE

The son of a dissident mother, Stanly Borque was punished for political crimes he didn't commit. Years later, he's a compliant corporate employee, working in the midst of the same authoritarian system his mother had hoped to eradicate. Which doesn't actually bother him too much—until a business trip to Ghana where a bizarre accident catapults him back into the world of the powerful.

A ubiquitous software company begins construction on a massive new corporate headquarters at the heart of Grid. At the same time, the legal rights to a dying woman's head are called into question. Two interlocking conspiracies are converging on a budding uppers addict, an informational psychopath, and schizotypal soda factory worker who believes he's a fish.

Cole Scott-Knox-Under, an idealistic technophobe purposefully relegating himself to a minimum-wage fast food job, suddenly notices he is suffering from a strange neurosis: inanimate objects appear to be speaking to him, and the symptoms are worsening. Hallucinations of a holocaust of waste threaten to sever him from his family, friends, and job. Or are they hallucinations at all?

3RD & ORANGE
JOSHUA PERALTA

In 2003, a young man arrives in Long Beach, CA searching for his voice as a writer. In the midst of college, he stumbles into a blissful but brief relationship. But at a time when nothing lasts long, the smallest details can lead to the longest-lasting impressions. Told first in poetry then in prose, a work of nostalgic force and painfully belated insights dedicated to the lingering presence of a lost love and the city in which it was born.

DEATH BY RAINBOW
DOC BASTARD

The graphic novel gold-standard for cyberpunk soap opera, anarcho-crime how-to, rollicking dimension-traipsers, and people behaving fucking badly. In the first issue, *Love Is A Dead Place*, the Stem system crashes, a gang war erupts in the lawless non-state of Babylon, and the underground sound sensation The Rainbow Princesses must navigate rehearsal, each other, and a tsunami of ultraviolence.